Embracing Danger

Two broken hearts…

Shane Anderson knows how much a broken heart hurts. Since the moment she left he's made it a point to never be emotionally vulnerable with a woman ever again. Not that it's helped much. He thinks about her every day.

Arden Cavendish has made more than a few bad decisions in life and coming back home after her divorce just might be the biggest. She's never stopped loving Shane and there's no way she's going to be able to avoid him in this little town. Keeping up the façade of indifference might be more than she handle.

A mystery from the past…

When Arden's father goes missing, she has no choice but to turn to Shane and his family for help finding him. With his shady business and double-dealings, she's terrified her father is in mortal danger. But their search has barely begun when she finds out her father's disappearance is only the tip of the iceberg as devastating secrets from her past are revealed.

Thankfully, Shane is there to offer a shoulder to lean on and strong arms to hold her. How can she tell her heart not to get too used to it?

Embracing Danger

Danger Incorporated

Book Four

BY

OLIVIA JAYMES

www.OliviaJaymes.com

Chapter One

ANOTHER PARTY, ANOTHER worthy charity, and another chance for vapid conversation with people Shane Anderson barely knew. Funny how they always seemed to know him. They'd slap him on the back, smile and laugh, then ask him what he'd been doing since they last saw him.

He had no idea.

He didn't remember the first time he'd met them, if he truly had at all. These weren't his friends or even acquaintances. Usually they were people that wanted something – money, influence, favors, sex, or just the opportunity to say they were good friends with an Anderson.

That and a dollar would get them a cup of coffee at the corner diner.

He had no illusions what the woman on his arm this evening wanted. Cassie Bowden was a long-legged brunette who liked to wrap those limbs around his waist while he pounded her into the mattress. To say that she was enthusiastic about their carnal pursuits was a dire understatement. The woman was voracious.

"I guess the rumors are true." Cassie squeezed his arm to get his attention. "I wasn't sure but here she is."

"Who are you talking about?"

Cassie did this quite a bit, starting in the middle of a conversation as if he'd been privy to her thoughts before she began to speak. It was annoying but at least he didn't work for her. She had to drive the employees of her real estate business insane if she did the same to them.

His companion nodded over to a throng of people gathered around the woman he hadn't seen in a long time. On purpose. "Arden Cavendish, of course. She's divorced and back in Tremont. She took a substitute teaching job at the high school hoping for a full time position next year. She even bought a house off of Old Pony Road that she's having renovated." Cassie wrinkled her nose disdainfully. "She used another real estate agent. I could have negotiated a better price for her. Well, her loss."

Arden was back in Tremont. People in hell must have been pulling on parkas and ice skates. He'd never thought to see the day.

"You shouldn't gossip," Shane replied automatically, his gaze glued to Arden. She hadn't aged a bit since the last time he'd seen her…about three years ago or so. She didn't come to Tremont often in the last decade, usually only for holidays so it was a shock to his system to see her tonight. He hadn't been expecting it so he hadn't had time to prepare properly.

Cassie simply laughed at him, running her manicured fingertips across his jaw playfully.

"It's not gossip if it's true. I thought you'd be interested as your families have always been such enemies. Benjamin Cavendish is through in local politics thanks to your brother West, and now his daughter is back in town minus a husband. Let's face it, that's the most exciting thing to happen in this one horse town in months."

Shane dragged his gaze from Arden and back to his date, giving her his most charming smile, the one that made panties drop and good women turn bad. "The Cavendish family doesn't really interest me, but if you want to talk about what might happen later this evening that's a topic I can get behind."

With a throaty giggle, Cassie lightly slapped his shoulder and her eyes darkened with lust. She was a sweet woman with more than her share of ambition, which made her perfect for Shane. She was all about her career, and the care and feeding of the male animal was not high on her list of wants.

"Shane Anderson, you are a naughty boy. Sexy but naughty. Is there any woman in this room you haven't been to bed with?"

Shrugging carelessly, he found himself looking again at Arden who was now standing much closer to him, just a few feet away.

"I think you like me this way. In fact, I know you do. As for the women here, does it really matter? I'm not husband material, we both know that, so my sexual history isn't really an issue."

"You'd make a lousy husband."

Her tone was caustic but she spoke the truth.

"Damn straight."

Cassie looked up at him, her mascaraed eyes narrowing dangerously. "Someday you're going to meet a woman and you won't be able to help yourself. You'll fall in love and – if there is any justice in the world – she'll break your cold, black heart."

Been there. Done that.

"We both know what this is, babe. Let's not pretend it's anything more."

Her fingers drew circles on the fabric of his suit jacket. "I don't care about the women in the past. You know that. And I don't care about the women in the future when you and I are through. I only care about the here and now, Shane. When a man's with me, he's with only me." She looked up at him, her hand sliding across his chest to rest over his heart. "Can you honestly say you've had better sex? I doubt it."

He took a step back so her hand fell back down to her side. He liked Cassie but he didn't like feeling she was trying to saddle him, even if it was only for a short time. He didn't play that game.

And he could say he'd had better sex.

"Go powder your nose, Cassie, before you say something we'll both regret. Then come back out here and dance with me."

Her fingers tightened on the champagne flute in her hand but she nodded in agreement, her posture relaxing and a smile returning to her face. "That's a good idea. Please excuse me."

The party was being held in the local theatre and the room was packed with people, the cloying scent of perfume and musty old props mixing together in a mad-scientist brew that drove him out of the main room and into the dressing room area behind the stage. He breathed in a lungful of air and only then realized he wasn't standing there alone.

Act normally. Don't let her see you sweat. You're past this.

"Arden." He inclined his head stiffly, his brain telling him to flee but his feet weren't listening. "I didn't realize you were here."

"I needed some space." Her fingers twisted around the leather of her small handbag. She wasn't as at ease as she tried to appear. "It's a little overwhelming in there."

"Welcome back to Tremont."

If she was thinking he was going to show any emotion or weakness, she would be disappointed. Too many years had passed and he'd learned to move on and survive without her. Barely.

"Thank you, Shane. It's good to be back." Her voice was husky and a little hesitant, probably wanting out of this conversation as much as he did but their manners had been drilled into them from childhood. They'd make small talk for a few minutes no matter how tortuous.

"I hear you took a teaching job at the high school."

Her hand fluttered to her throat and her cheeks turned a shade of pink. "That is what I trained for."

His gaze flickered to her bare ring finger and she curled her hand into a fist and shoved it behind her back, her body language betraying her agitation.

"You only taught for a few years. I assumed you didn't enjoy it."

"I was doing other things." She shifted on her feet like she wanted to bolt at any moment, her own gaze darting everywhere but at him. "I hear you're a big shot in Anderson Industries now."

He didn't want to talk about himself or how he'd spent his time since she'd left town.

"What other things were you doing? Did hubby not like you to work?"

She stiffened at his dig and her chin lifted slightly. This was more the Arden he remembered. This mild-mannered, soft-spoken debutante barely resembled the young woman he'd spent a sun-drenched summer with.

"I don't think it's any of your business, Shane. And asking about it is rude, by the way."

"It was honest, or don't you care about that anymore? Are you your father's daughter completely now, princess?"

He hadn't stood this close to Arden in over a decade but his body responded as if he were that twenty-two year old besotted young man all over again. She'd always had that effect on him from the first moment he'd laid eyes on her.

Gorgeous as always, tonight she was wearing a black cocktail dress with some sort of rhinestones around the neckline and hem. Her mouth-watering legs were shown off to perfection by the sky-high black pumps she wore, although they did little to help her see over the crowd. She'd always been a tiny thing and high heels weren't going to change that much. Her blonde hair was piled on top of her head in a mass of curls, a few falling down to brush the petal soft skin of her face.

Her lips tightened into a thin line, but then he'd always known what buttons to push. "You just can't leave my father out of this, can you? He doesn't have anything to do with this."

"Keep telling yourself that and you might start to believe it." Shane stepped toward the back door, not enjoying this exchange in the least. Too much had gone on between them to make nice now. As it was, memories were crowding his mind making it difficult to think clearly. "Good night, Arden. Enjoy your new job."

It was time to get the hell out of here. The party was only

pissing him off and this woman was a big reason. He was normally quite sociable but tonight he wanted to be alone with his thoughts and a longneck.

He burst out of the back door of the theatre, the chilly wind biting at his skin. It slapped him in the face and woke him up from the unreality of the last few minutes with Arden. He'd never thought to see her move back but now she had. He needed to decide what that meant for him.

Or if it even mattered.

Of course it did. It changed everything.

He rubbed the back of his neck and turned to go in and find Cassie, but a figure stood in the doorway. Benjamin Cavendish blocked the entrance, his expression familiar to Shane. It was the same one he'd worn the night Shane had learned that Arden had gone back east to school.

"Ben."

"Shane." Ben moved closer but still kept a few feet between them. "I saw Arden come back to the main room and I wondered who she was talking to. I should have known it was you. I'm surprised you waited this long, honestly."

Shane's jaw ached as he gritted his teeth together, hate for this man churning in his gut. He disliked few people, but Ben Cavendish was right up there on the list and for so much more than what he'd done to Shane and Arden.

"Still spying on your daughter, Ben? Seems like she's old enough to run her own life now. She's a grown woman."

"I'm a parent who cares." Cavendish pointed his finger at Shane, his demeanor bordering on threatening but Shane wasn't afraid of this man. He'd already done his worst. "There's no point in you sniffing around her again. She's getting back together with her husband."

"Does she know that? Because she's got a job and bought a house, Ben. Not the actions of a woman looking to reunite with the hubby you hand-picked."

Unless she was simply trying to make her husband jealous.

"She and Michael are the perfect couple." Cavendish took another step forward. "She doesn't give a shit about you anymore, Anderson. How does it feel? Do you still dream about her at night? She doesn't give you a second thought."

"You've invaded her thoughts as well? Jesus, Ben, you're getting paranoid in your old age. You don't even want poor Arden to have dreams. The woman I knew wouldn't have appreciated that."

"The woman you knew left," Ben spat, his cheeks stained crimson as anger took over. "Even if she wasn't getting back with Michael, how could she ever be with you again? Look at what you've become. A rich playboy with a different woman every night. She couldn't respect you or love you. Stay away from Arden, Shane. She's not for you. She was never…for you."

Cavendish whirled on his heel and strode back into the theatre but Shane stood rooted to the spot despite the rapidly falling temperature outside. This night had gone downhill quickly and he needed to leave before he did or said something that would absolutely only make things worse.

Heading to find Cassie and leave, he nodded to a few donors along the way, determined to get out of the theatre without getting waylaid by anyone else. The polite veneer he wore at events like this was quickly peeling away and he needed to vacate the premises before anyone saw the raw man underneath. Running into Arden tonight was too much. He hadn't been prepared for it.

Seeing her was like a knife to his heart.

Chapter Two

TREMBLING WITH EMOTION, Arden struggled to open her car door, her fingers slipping on the handle before succeeding in climbing into the vehicle. She sat there for a long time, taking deep breaths to calm her racing heart but her body wouldn't cooperate.

She'd seen Shane. She'd talked to him although that hadn't worked out so well. She'd wondered how long she would be back in town before she ran into him and now she had her answer. Not long. Back only a few weeks, she hadn't been prepared for the storm of conflicting feelings that swamped her when she'd laid eyes on him tonight.

He looked good as always, a few strands of silver at his temples and a couple of lines around his eyes. Time looked good on him, she had to admit. He clearly had improved with age.

"Don't think about him," Arden muttered to herself, exhausted after an evening of answering the same questions over and over. Everyone was naturally curious as to why she'd come home but her patience was beginning to wear thin. "Concentrate on getting your life back."

Her psyche needed the pep talk. It had been a long, crappy

year with the divorce and frankly, she was looking forward to starting over with a new home and a new job. She was glad to be close to her beloved grandmother although it also put her into close proximity with her father, their relationship the definition of complicated. She was living with him at the moment while her new home was being remodeled but hopefully only for a short time. She needed her independence from Benjamin Cavendish. If it was up to him he'd control every aspect of her life down to her friends and job.

Turning right onto the dark, deserted private two lane road that led to her father's house, Arden didn't let herself dwell on her meeting with Shane. The future was all she could control and she was excited about her new life.

Slowing the vehicle as she approached a sharp corner, she reached out and turned the radio on and the car flooded with happy tunes from the oldies station. A flash of headlights had her squinting as she came onto the straight part of the road. The car opposite had their brights on and she could barely see a few feet in front of her. Instinct had her decelerating, but the other vehicle was upon her before she could stop completely.

Those same blinding headlights were now coming straight at her in her own lane at a frightening speed. She barely had time to mutter a curse before jerking the wheel to the left, hoping the driver would stay in her lane while she occupied his rightful one so she could go around him safely.

Her adrenaline surged and she turned much too sharply, pushing her two left tires into the loose gravel on the side of the road. Her heart jumped into her throat as the vehicle skidded and only a death grip on the wheel kept it from spinning in the other direction. Just when she thought she was out of danger, the tires caught the firmer ground and the car barreled forward, straight at a cluster of trees. She slammed on the brake but not before her bumper came into hard contact with one of the immoveable tree trunks.

An object flew at her face, knocking her back into her seat and pushing the oxygen from her lungs. She sat there for a long time, letting her breathing and heart rate return to normal. The airbag had deployed on impact and she had slight red marks on her hands from the chemicals. A quick inventory of her limbs and head let her know she was dazed but unhurt.

Blinking tears away, she was able to locate her handbag, hooking it on her shoulder before stumbling from the car. The front of the car was smashed in and would probably need to be towed. Sighing, she locked the vehicle and looked up the long road and then down at her already aching feet, encased in gold Jimmy Choo sandals with a three inch heel.

The half mile walk to the house was going to hugely suck. In fact, the entire evening had been a disaster. She couldn't wait to crawl into a bathtub and soak her cares away.

FLINGING HER PURSE onto the couch, Arden fell into the inviting cushions, groaning in relief. Her feet had already been sore from dancing at the party and the half mile hike hadn't helped that situation. Her heels were rubbed raw and her arches were screaming for mercy as she slid the expensive sandals off her feet, letting them fall to the floor with a satisfying thud. She rubbed her frozen toes, trying to get the circulation back into her chilled to the bone feet and pains shot through the soles as the blood began to flow again.

"Shit," she muttered. "Next time I wear boots. The kind with furry linings and flat heels."

Leaning back and closing her eyes, she found the silence in the house comforting after an evening of music and chatter with people she barely remembered, if at all. Most of them had been more curious about her than anything, and she'd tried to keep a smile on her face even during the most humiliating questions regarding her divorce.

Nothing like being a sideshow this evening.

Then the whole fiasco with Shane hadn't made things much better. He was bitter and he had a reason to be, but she'd assumed that he'd moved on and didn't care much anymore. She'd kept discreet tabs on him over the years and he'd become quite the playboy with a different woman on his arm every night. Honestly she'd assumed he barely remembered their summer so long ago and had often wondered if perhaps it only had meaning to her. They'd both been so young.

But she'd never forgotten. That brief time had haunted her even as she'd married another man. No male could measure up to Shane but she'd known that when she left.

Her shoes hooked in her fingers, she slowly stood, her back popping and cracking in a few places. She'd been caught by several people on her way out of the party so her father had ducked out before her, but there didn't seem to be any sign that he'd returned home. Normally he turned on the television in the study saying he liked the noise in the background, but the house was eerily quiet. Padding on bare feet, she stuck her head into the garage to check for his car. Perhaps he'd stopped somewhere on his way home.

The dark luxury sedan was sitting in its usual spot.

He was probably already upstairs asleep.

Entering her own room, she flipped on her bedside lamp and tossed her shoes in the bottom of her closet. It would be a long while before she'd wear them again after the torture of tonight. She stripped off her dress and hung it up before wrapping a robe around her body and tightly tying the sash. She worked on the pins in her hair as she walked back into the bathroom.

Tomorrow would be a new day and she'd start fresh. She'd talked to Shane and survived. It hadn't been easy but she'd known it wouldn't be. He was angry, and rightfully so, but even if she told him why she'd really left would it make any difference? Nothing had changed.

She'd tried so hard to put him behind her, to forget him, but Shane wasn't a man easily forgotten.

And clearly he couldn't forgive.

Humming a song from that fateful summer, Arden stopped in front of the mirror to see a folded piece of paper propped up against her toothbrush holder. She unfolded it and quickly scanned the brief contents.

Arden,

I'll be out of town for awhile. Please don't worry.

Love,
Your father

Out of town? For sure, he hadn't mentioned any trips. She

would have remembered that. In fact, he'd talked about having a welcome home party for her in a few weeks. Whatever this trip was it had come up at the last minute.

She walked back into the bedroom and picked up the landline on the bedside table and dialed her father's cell, listening as it rang and rang before going to voicemail. She left a message to call her as soon as possible, surprised her father hadn't answered. His phone was like another appendage and he was never without it. He depended on it for medication alarms, appointments, and contact numbers. He'd been one of the first people to embrace having a mobile phone and she often teased him that he loved it like a child.

Something didn't feel right.

He wasn't answering his phone.

But his car was in the garage.

His note didn't give her any details.

And why had he even written a note? Normally if he had something to tell her he'd either say it in person or send her a text. He'd seen her less than an hour ago, after all, and nothing had seemed amiss.

A quick glance at the clock told her it was too late to call Dexter, her father's attorney and best friend. If Ben Cavendish was taking care of any sort of business Dexter would know about it. She'd call him in the morning and get the details. In the meantime, she'd remind herself that her father was a grown man and could take care of himself. He'd specifically said not to worry. But that only made her worry more.

Chapter Three

S HANE'S STOMACH WAS rumbling as he pushed open the
door to the local sports bar the next day, the smell of
charred meat and melted cheese wrapping around him. After a
long morning of paperwork, he was meeting his brothers for
lunch, an Anderson family tradition actually started at the behest
of their mother who wanted them to remain close no matter how
their lives might diverge.

They'd eat some artery clogging grub, drink a few beers,
maybe flirt with a cute waitress, and generally catch up with the
latest news. All four brothers tried to make it but every now and
then something did come up. But this time, they would all be
there.

His brothers were waiting for him at a table near the back
but close enough to the televisions to watch the college football
games. Shane shrugged off his jacket and hung it on the back of
his chair while he signaled to Jackie the waitress for a beer.

"Christ, the temperature really dropped last night. Yesterday
felt like a summer day and today I'm freezing my nuts off,"
Shane observed with a shiver. "I wish the weather would make
up its mind."

A longneck was slid in front of him and he thanked Jackie with a smile. They'd dated a few years back but were now just friends. No hard feelings. She had a boyfriend over in Springwood that worked at the Perry ranch.

"You boys know what you want?" she asked, a hand on her hip. She was a pretty girl with auburn hair and long legs, but she also had a bad habit of drinking with her girlfriends and drunk dialing him at three in the morning.

"Or do you need some time?"

They'd been coming there for years and knew the menu by heart. Shane had known last week what he was going to have. All four brothers ordered and Jackie swayed back to the kitchen, Carter's gaze on the woman's ass.

"Jackie's looking really good these days. Maybe you and she should spark something up again."

Shane snorted into his beer. "Only if I can confiscate her cell whenever she goes out. She's a sloppy drunk, my brother. But you're welcome to find out for yourself. She's given you the eye more than once."

"No, thanks. I'd like a woman who hasn't fallen under the spell of my older brother."

Noah, the eldest son by seven minutes, choked and coughed. "That's going to cut down on female candidates, little brother. Shane here is making his way through the female population like a buzz saw. Better grab one while you can."

Carter gave Shane a sour look. "Find one woman and settle down, for fuck's sake. You're going to be forty soon. You're starting to look creepy with a different woman on your arm every weekend."

An image of Arden in a scarlet bikini splashing around in the pool by moonlight flashed through Shane's mind, but he shoved that memory away as quickly as it had come up. That was old news and they'd both moved on. She'd moved so far that she'd up and married some other guy.

Shane grabbed a few pretzels from the basket in the middle of the table and lobbed one at Carter. "I'll find one when I'm good and ready. Your woman problems are not my issue."

Easton, the more serious brother and twin to Noah, heaved a long sigh. "Stop bickering. Christ on a crutch, don't you all have anything better to talk about than Shane's addiction to females? It's a worn-out topic."

"So pick a new one," Noah replied easily. "Anything interesting going on?"

Carter took a swig of his beer and slapped it down on the table, giving Shane a side-eyed look. "Arden Cavendish was in West's office this morning raising hell. Apparently she can't find her father and she's worried. He left a note that he was leaving town for a while but he's not answering his phone and Dexter Lowell doesn't know where he is either, and that's strange as hell. Cavendish's car is in the garage but he's nowhere to be found. She went to the police but they told her he wasn't a missing person until he'd been gone for seventy-two hours, plus he left a note so technically he's not missing in the eyes of the law. I guess she thought West might put some pressure on them to open an investigation. She looked and sounded frantic, said she knew something isn't right."

Shane's fingers flexed around the cold bottle but he deliberately kept his features schooled. His brothers were aware that he'd dated Arden but they didn't know all the details. He wanted to keep it that way, if possible.

"Where does she think her father is?"

"That's the interesting thing. She had no idea. He was at the party last night and now he's gone with only a two sentence note telling her he was leaving. I guess someone also ran her off the private road to their house last night, so she had to walk the last half mile. No one should be on that road unless they're visiting the Cavendish place."

One thing Shane knew was the Arden of the past hadn't been a hysterical female, so hearing that she was upset and worried about her father had him wondering if she might be right.

"What were you and West doing at the office this morning?" Easton asked. "It is Saturday."

"No rest when you're working on a big project," Carter laughed. "We had some last minute details on the teen center to discuss and it was the only time we were both free. We should be able to schedule the open house before the holidays."

Carter ran the construction arm of Anderson Industries and he was heading up West's pet project as mayor – a new teen center, which had been built completely from donations.

Shane sat back in his chair, crossing his legs, not wanting to appear as if the answer was important to him. "Does West know anything about who ran Arden off the road?"

Carter shook his head. "It was too dark so she didn't see any-thing and there were no witnesses. He's got the police looking at the traffic light footage a few miles up the road. They might find something there."

Noah frowned. "So what does Arden want West to do exactly? Run Ben's credit cards and see if he's charged something somewhere?"

"That's one place to start," Carter replied. "Let's face it, Cavendish ran with some unsavory characters, so Arden has a reason to be concerned if you ask me. Maybe one of his business associates finally got tired of his shit."

Shane shook his head. "Listen, I don't like the bastard any more than you do. Hell, I have more than a few reasons to hate his guts. but if anything happens to him Arden is going to be heartbroken. She loves him, although I don't know why."

Easton pointed a fork at Shane. "He's her father, dumbass. It doesn't have to make sense, it just is. But I agree with Carter, she has reason to worry. He's been elbow deep in illegal shit for years, except nobody could prove it. It may have caught up to him."

How many times had Shane tried to convince Arden that her father had made his money with deals that weren't always above board? She'd been adamant that he was lying and they'd had more than a few arguments about her unflinching loyalty to a man that Shane knew was as crooked as Blue Mill Road.

"So what did West say? Is he going to help her?"

Carter shrugged and picked at the label of his longneck. "He said he'd run her daddy's credit cards and put out a BOLO for him. But he pointed out that Ben is a grown man, left a note, and doesn't have to check in with his daughter, especially since she's been in New York all this time. For all she knows, he does this every now and then. He doesn't have to answer to anyone."

Their food came right after, and in between bites Shane

heard about the latest headaches on the ranch from Noah and some issues that had come up with the financial investments with Easton. Every Anderson male had a job to do to keep the family business running smoothly. Only the lone female Leann had escaped the pull of Anderson Industries.

They paid their bill and headed out into the chilly air. Shane bid his brothers goodbye and headed to his motorcycle but he quickly realized Easton was on his tail.

"Are you going to be okay?"

Shane wanted to pretend he didn't know what his older brother was talking about. "Why wouldn't I be?"

"Don't be obtuse. I'm talking about Arden. She's back and you're going to be seeing a lot of her."

Leaning against the parking meter, Shane played with the keys, his gaze on the tip of his boots. Easton and Noah were old enough to know he'd dated Arden that summer but they didn't know everything that had gone on. They just thought they did.

"It was a long time ago, East, and best left in the past. When I see her, I'll be polite and cordial. I hope she does the same. But that's it. I'm not looking to rekindle anything if that's what you're thinking. Those days are over."

The woman he saw last night probably didn't have much in common with the girl he'd loved so many years ago, although he'd seen a flash of the past when she'd got her back up.

But Daddy said she was going back to her ex-husband. Shane doubted it was true but then Ben Cavendish could be mighty persuasive when he wanted to be.

"She's divorced now."

"So?" Shane challenged, straightening up and looking his

brother in the eye. "Is that what you think I've been doing all these years? Pining and waiting for my chance to pounce? I can assure you that's not the case. We had a summer fling. End of story."

I am such a fucking liar.

Easton regarded Shane steadily, no smile on his face, but then he was the most serious of all the sons. "Is that what you've told yourself? You haven't been the same since she left town."

"I grew the hell up." Shane picked up the helmet and pulled it over his head. "Love is a fairy tale, big brother. It's an illusion created by mirrors, lights, and alcohol. I might have believed in it once but I'm not that naive anymore."

"Jesus, Shane. You are one cynical asshole. Is there anything you do believe in?"

Shane laughed and fired up the cycle, a 1965 Harley Electra Glide he'd restored with his own two hands. "Hell, yes. I believe in me, our family, and an honest day's work. Oh, and I also believe in karma, although I don't get to witness it nearly enough. So actually, I believe in quite a bit. What do you believe in?"

"I believe you've been lying to yourself for so long you don't know what the truth is anymore."

There were no words left to say. Shane wasn't angry with Easton; he'd only meant well, but an argument on the sidewalk of Tremont wasn't going to change anyone's mind.

Now all Shane had to do was convince himself that he didn't love Arden anymore.

Chapter Four

ARDEN'S GRANDMOTHER'S HOME was as formal as the woman who lived in it. Dark cherry wood, heavy woven rugs, and original paintings on the walls gave the home an uncomfortable feeling, like those scratchy dresses with the crinolines that Arden had been forced to wear on holidays so she could pose for pictures and be shown off like a prize cow.

Arden was sure her grandmother had never worn a pair of jeans in her entire life. Even now in her late seventies, she was dressed in an off-white Chanel suit with her silver hair meticulously coiffed and her face tastefully made up. Elaine Graham had been a beauty in her day and was still a handsome woman who attracted attention when she attended a social event or traveled. In fact, there was a rumor that an older Greek millionaire had proposed marriage just last summer.

Of course he had been tactfully turned down and sent on his way. Elaine often said that she was too old and set in her ways to shoehorn a man in her life at this juncture.

Arden carefully lifted the antique ceramic teapot with the ring of pink roses and poured two cups of tea, one for her and the other for her grandmother, who was currently sitting on the damask settee in her parlor room.

That her grandmother even had a parlor room had always amused Arden to no end. Elaine had been brought up with wealth and that meant homes that were photographed for glossy magazines. Homes like that had parlors.

"Arden Amelia, when will you remember that you add the milk first and then the tea?"

Elaine had spent several years in London with her husband and to this day was quite passionate about her tea rituals. She'd also acquired a bit of a British accent, which she zealously held onto in memory of her late "darling Charles".

Arden smiled at the scolding. "Sorry, Grandmother. I'll do better next time."

Her grandmother sat back with her delicate china cup and sighed. "I'm sure you will. So tell me what the police and West Anderson said. He runs a tight ship in this town. Much better than your father ever did, I must say."

And there it was. Elaine Graham couldn't stand Ben Cavendish and never missed an opportunity to say so. She'd begged her only daughter not to marry him but to no avail.

"They said that Dad isn't missing if he left a note, plus I have to wait seventy-two hours before filing a missing persons report anyway. I told West that Dad's car was still in the garage and that he wasn't answering his phone but he didn't think that was anything to worry about."

"Hmmm…he has a point, dear. Your father is an adult, and if he wants to run off to God knows where for some secret reason he can do that. He doesn't have to tell you every detail of his life."

Arden was aware but she couldn't stop the worried feeling in her gut telling her that something was very wrong.

"I know that…" Arden trailed off, not wanting her grandmother to think she was overreacting but in truth she felt she was *under-reacting*. "It's just he always answers his phone, no matter what, no matter where. I've been calling since last night and…nothing."

Elaine's expression softened and reached across the coffee table to pat Arden's hand, a miraculous show of affection for the old woman. "I can see why you'd be concerned. Was West no help at all?"

"He said he'd run Daddy's credit cards and see if he had used them to go somewhere. He also said he'd have the police talk to the local cab service. They might have taken him to the airport."

"It sounds like West is doing all he can. Is there something else you wanted the police to do?"

Frustrated, Arden fiddled with her tea cup. She wasn't ungrateful for West's help but she'd hoped for more. "I guess I just wanted them to care a little bit. They acted like it was no big deal and that I was worried for nothing."

"Maybe you are," Elaine suggested gently.

"No, I know there's more to this. There's something going on."

Her grandmother appeared to be searching for the right words. "Your father hasn't always done business ethically. He's made enemies along the way."

It had taken years for Arden to admit that fact. She and Shane had fought so many times about that very subject. She owed him a big, fat apology because he'd been right about so many things.

"I know, and that's what I'm afraid of. I don't even know that Daddy wrote that note since it was printed off of the computer. Anyone could have written it and then taken him somewhere."

"All the more reason for you to stay out of it. If someone 'helped' him leave then it's dangerous for you to go poking around, child. Stay out of it."

"How can I? He's my father, no matter what he's done."

Setting the cup back on the table, Elaine nodded. "I suppose if you're that worried you could ask for private help."

"Private? I'm not sure I follow you."

Steepling her fingers, the older woman sat back in the cushions of the settee. "Shane's cousin West is a former cop, his other cousin Jason is a former federal agent. Plus, he has all sorts of law enforcement connections that might be able to find your father for you. But you'd have to ask, of course."

Elaine couldn't possibly be suggesting what Arden thought she was. It was idiotic. Insane. Crazy. And a few other synonyms she couldn't come up with at the moment but might later.

"I cannot ask Shane to help me, Grandmother."

"Why not? You two were quite close once."

Arden groaned and rolled her eyes. "Sure, before I left him. Let's not even discuss how our families can't stand each other. Why on God's green earth would Shane want to help me find Daddy?"

"Shane cared about you. Did things go badly when you saw him at the party last night?"

They hadn't invented words yet that described how poorly

their meeting had gone. Arden had handled it all wrong but at the same time she didn't know what she would have done differently.

"I don't know. I was scared and excited too. But there was a sense of dread because although I've seen him at a distance over the years, I'd never spoken to him until the night of the party. He's…bitter."

"He has reason to be, I think. I doubt Benjamin was kind when he told him you left."

"The Andersons weren't happy either about him dating me–"

"Pish posh," Elaine interrupted, her scowl demonstrating in no uncertain terms she didn't want to hear excuses for Arden's father. "You may not have been their first choice but they never intervened. Not like *him*. He had to have everything his own way."

Arden sipped her rapidly cooling tea. She had no words of defense – not for him or for herself. She was just as culpable as Ben Cavendish.

"I just need to try and stay away from him."

"That sounds like the worst idea in the world, my child. I doubt you'll be able to achieve that goal in a small town like this. It would be best if you and Shane Anderson sat down and talked this all out. Cleared the air, so to speak. I'm sure he's moved on emotionally. My question is…have you?"

"I've been married, Grandmother. Doesn't that sound like moving on?"

Chuckling, Elaine picked up a small cookie from the delicate plate on the tray. "It depends on whom you marry, I suppose.

How is that bastard Michael? Still screwing his secretary?"

Tea definitely wasn't strong enough for this conversation. Arden needed alcohol to withstand her grandmother's blunt questioning.

"I have no idea. He was when I caught him that day in his office. Whether he continued to do so is his own business now. He says he's in love." Arden slapped the cup down on the table. "Father wants us to reconcile."

Elaine's lips curled in distaste. "Your father is a heartless idiot. If he loves Michael so much maybe he should marry him. But if you were thinking of perhaps taking that snake back, let me tell you, young lady, I will write you out of my will. I can call my estate attorney right now."

"I'm not going to take him back, not that I want your money. I want you to live a very long time indeed."

Elaine sniffed delicately. "No one lives forever, my child. That's why you can't take a day for granted. Now back to the important topic at hand. What do you intend to do about Shane Anderson?"

Arden had assumed that subject was over with. "Nothing...I mean...it's all in the past. There's nothing...*to do*."

Elaine Graham leaned forward, her gaze trained on her only grandchild. "The past, my dear, has a way of rising from the grave. My query is what do you intend to do about that if it happens?"

Arden didn't have an answer, and she feared she never would.

Chapter Five

A LL SHANE WANTED to do was kick back and relax, maybe have a beer and read. He'd spent the better part of the afternoon in the office trying to get through a pile of paperwork but had made little progress. He'd spent too much time thinking about Arden.

As he drove down the pitch black lane to his log home on the outskirts of the Anderson ranch, he hit the remote clipped to his car's visor and a flood of lights came on as his garage door slowly creeped up, illuminating the house and the grounds. It was then that he saw the car parked in front of his house, the engine running but the lights off. Tensing, he pulled his car into the garage but didn't lower the door, his hand automatically reaching for the handgun he kept in the glove compartment. He kept his eye on the vehicle as he palmed the cold metal but then chuckled as Arden stepped from the car.

As nasty as they'd been to each other the night before, he was sure she wasn't here to rob or kill him. But that begged the question as to why was she here?

He swung out of the driver's seat and stood next to the SUV waiting for her to join him. She was wearing her hair down tonight and he had to quell the urge to reach for one of her curls and tug at it.

"I've been waiting for you, Shane."

She stopped right in front of him looking more beautiful than she had any right to. He'd spent the last fifteen years comparing every woman he'd ever met to her and none of them measured up. Arden wasn't beautiful in the classic sense; her chin was too short and her nose had a slight bump on it that he thought was cute, but she had that something that glowed from within. Shane didn't know what it was exactly, perhaps intelligence, humor, or simply a zest for life, but she had it in bucketloads and it meant that he'd never been able to forget her.

"I hope you didn't wait long." Shane jerked his head toward the door to the house. "Would you like to come in and tell me why you're here?"

It was a bad idea but he couldn't turn her away after she'd waited for him. They should stay far away from each other and they would. Tomorrow. He couldn't ignore the nagging ache inside that constantly chanted her name in his head and made him remember the good times they'd shared.

Following him into the house, she stood uncertainly in his kitchen before placing her handbag on the table and unbuttoning her coat. "I wasn't sure you'd let me in."

Shane grabbed two bottles from the refrigerator as she draped her coat over a chair. He opened the beers and offered one to her, watching her hesitate and then accept it with a small smile. "You thought I'd leave you out in the cold. That's not very chivalrous, Arden. I'm an asshole but not a jerk."

She pulled out a chair at the kitchen table and sank down

into it while he settled himself across from her. "I never thought you were, but you have to admit we weren't kind to one another at the party last night."

And that's something else he'd always loved about her. Arden had been the kindest person he'd ever met. People, animals, you name it. She'd had a soft heart and didn't bother to hide it.

"It was a shock seeing you. I wasn't prepared for it but I am now." He took a long swig of the icy cold beer. "So to what do I owe this unexpected pleasure?"

Her fingertips ran up and down the bottle and he inwardly shivered as images of the two of them besieged him...moans, caresses, hot summer nights, and hotter kisses. They'd never had a problem in the sex department, despite her inexperience.

She didn't answer right away, instead staring out the window into the darkness. She couldn't see a damn thing out there with the external lights off but that didn't seem to matter. He thought he was going to have to ask the question again when she finally answered, her blue eyes stormy.

"My father is missing."

Shane steeled himself, not allowing a flicker of reaction to cross his features. "Missing? Are you sure? I heard he left you a note that said he would be gone for a while. That doesn't sound like missing."

Arden shook her head and leaned forward, her palms flat on the table. "Something is very wrong, Shane. I know it. His car is in the garage but the cab company says they didn't pick him up. A vehicle ran me off of our private road when I was coming home from the party. Was my father in that car? Plus, the note wasn't handwritten. It was printed off of a computer—anyone could have written it. And finally Daddy isn't answering his cell phone. He's never done that. Ever. He loves that phone and he loves talking on it. If he's not answering it's not because he doesn't want to. It's because he can't."

Stroking his chin, Shane didn't answer right away. She'd made a few good points, especially about Ben's cell phone. The man's ear was sealed to the damn thing.

"Let's assume what you're saying is true. Someone else wrote that note and someone took your father from the house. Let's even say that he's being held against his will."

"Or worse," Arden interrupted, two spots of color on her pale cheeks. "It could be much worse."

He held his hand up to halt her words. "Easy, honey. I can see you've spent too much time thinking of all the worst-case scenarios. Chances are this is just Ben being a thoughtless asshole. Something your father excels at. You're letting your imagination scare you."

Pressing her lips together, she blinked a few times, her eyes bright with unshed tears.

"I know who and what my father is and that's why I'm concerned about him. He'd never leave the way he did of his own free will. I think something has happened to him and it's not just my imagination."

"So you're admitting that Ben is involved with some unsavory characters? After all these years I never thought to see the day."

Arden jumped up from where she was sitting to pace the kitchen. "Do you want me to say it? You were right, Shane, and I was wrong. My father has made some unethical and possibly illegal business deals." She took a deep breath and turned to face him. "There. Are you happy now? You get to be right."

"I wish I'd been wrong only because I know the truth had to come as a shock to you."

A smile played on her lips as she sat back down at the table. "Careful, Shane. You almost sounded nice for a moment. Like you forgot about the past."

Shane took a big slug from the longneck before he replied. "Actually I never want to forget something that has been so instructive in my life. I learned about human nature and it's been invaluable. Really, I should be thanking you."

His tone had been more caustic than he'd planned but he wasn't trying to win friends and influence people here. He was simply trying to get through this encounter with Arden with some sort of sanity intact. Dignity wouldn't be bad either.

"I suppose I am the villain in your story and I'm sorry that time has made you so cynical."

He took another drink of his beer and then slapped it down on the table, watching in satisfaction as Arden jumped at the sound. "So you haven't answered my first question, princess. To what do I owe the honor of this visit? It wasn't just to tell me Daddy took a powder, was it?"

Her lips trembled and her tongue darted out to wet them nervously as her hands twisted together in her lap. "I'm here...to...ask for your help."

His eyebrow quirked but he said nothing, giving her the floor to keep speaking. Her chin lifted and her knuckles turned white as her fingers gripped each other tightly.

"I'm asking for your help to find my father. I don't have anywhere else to turn."

He didn't know what he'd expected her to say but that wasn't it. It was his turn to stand and put some distance between the two of them. He leaned his hip against the stove and tried not to laugh. The entire situation was bordering on hilarious.

"You want me to help," he repeated calmly. "What about the police? That's their job."

"They won't do anything until he's been gone for seventy-two hours, and even then I don't think they're taking me seriously because of that note. I need someone to start looking now."

Not to mention most of the town would just as soon leave old Ben missing if they had a choice.

"Then hire a private investigator. I'm sure there's one that would be glad of the work."

Standing, Arden moved closer so she was looking up at him. He could smell the light floral and vanilla of her perfume and it made his gut contract painfully to gaze down into her pleading blue eyes.

"I could but I don't know who to trust, honestly. I know you have connections, Shane. You, West, Jason, and your brothers too. I need someone I can trust and that I know will be discreet no matter what we find."

His lips turned up at the corners. "You make me sound like some kind of secret spy. I'm a businessman, not a cop."

"I told Grandmother you'd say no." Arden was staring out of the window now, disappointment ringing clearly in her tone. "She insisted you'd say yes. She said you were the only person I could trust with this."

Elaine Graham was a formidable woman but Shane wouldn't have ever said he was close or even friendly with her. She lived in a large house just outside of town and didn't venture out much these days, although she had when she was younger. She'd never made a big deal about Shane dating Arden but he hadn't thought she was on their side either.

"Listen," he began carefully, not wanting to upset Arden any more than she already was but needing to put an end to this request. She was asking too much. "I know you're upset and worried. But you need to let the police do their job before jumping to any conclusions. Ben is probably just off with a lady friend or something. He'll be home in a week or so with a big smile on his face and everything will be fine."

It was true he knew people that could be helpful and he was more than capable of leading an investigation, but if he agreed to this he'd be around her, immersed in her world. He wasn't sure he could survive being that close to her without breaking.

Arden turned and began shrugging on her coat, studiously avoiding looking at him. He had a sinking feeling she was crying and her tears had always been his kryptonite. "I'm sure you're right. I'll go before you have to throw me out. I'm sorry I bothered you."

Now he felt like shit. "You're not bothering me and I'd never throw you out, princess. I just think you need to give this a little time to shake out, that's all."

Her back was facing him as she slipped her purse strap over her shoulder. "Thank you for listening anyway. I…need to go now."

She walked quickly out the same garage door she'd come in

with Shane right at her heels and feeling about two inches tall. A part of him wanted to help her but dammit, he just couldn't without ripping his heart into pieces again.

She was halfway out of the garage when she stopped abruptly, her hand reaching out to run her fingers over the chrome handlebars of his cycle, a small smile on her face.

Even after all these years, she remembered.

"You still have it."

He came to stand beside her and patted the leather seat. "This is a different one, but I did the restoration on this one myself as well. I'm trying to get as much riding time in as I can before the snow comes."

They were both thinking back to those hot summer rides down to the lake. Skinny-dipping and then making love in the moonlight. Kisses and whispers. Passion and giggles. It had been everything and then it was gone.

"What happened to your old one?"

"Wrecked," he said flatly. "I laid it down when a car turned in front of me. Broke my wrist in two places and got a lecture from Mom so blistering that I can still hear it echoing in my brain. She was madder than a wet hen and begged me not to replace it. But of course I did as soon as I was healed enough to ride again."

"Your mother hated that bike."

"She hates this one just as much," Shane assured her. "Maybe more because now she says I should have the good sense not to ride. She's probably right. When was the last time you rode, princess?"

Her hand jerked away from the cycle as if she'd been burned.

"With you," she whispered before turning on her heel and heading straight for her vehicle.

Emotion that he had long buried clawed at his heart, making itself known. Images that he thought he had forgotten flooded his consciousness, almost bringing him to his knees with their power. There was a time in his life when he could refuse this woman nothing.

He hadn't changed, although he would have sworn he had. He would have told everyone that he'd moved on and his heart was mended. He'd lied.

"Wait," he heard himself saying, knowing he'd regret it later. "I'll help you. Not a full blown investigation but I'll make a few inquiries, okay?"

Arden whirled around and for the first time he saw hope in her expression. "You mean it? You'll really help me?"

He was an idiot and this female could tie him in knots without breaking a sweat. He'd known his answer to her request at the beginning and had only been fighting the inevitable. Turning her away was a non-starter. Sadly, he had a deep-seated and pathetic need to be her knight in shining armor.

"I'll check around but I can't promise anything. Understand?"

If Ben was holed up in a hotel somewhere with a couple of hookers and a case of gin, Shane was going to kick his ass for worrying Arden like this.

"I understand. Thank you."

"Don't thank me yet," Shane warned. "You may not like what I dig up."

"I'll take my chances. I'm so grateful that you're doing this."

The last thing he wanted was her gratitude.

"Go home, and if I find anything I'll call you."

He watched as she climbed into her car and left, her taillights fading into the darkness. Chilled, he went back into the house and stood in the center of the kitchen, his brain trying to comprehend his own stupidity. He'd agreed to help Arden and he couldn't change his mind now. Racing for his cell, he swiped the screen and pressed a few buttons.

"West? It's Shane. I need to talk to you about this Ben Cavendish thing. Can we meet? Yeah, that's sounds good. I'll meet you at the diner in thirty. Thanks."

Pressing the end button, he reached for the keys to the cycle. It was colder than a witch's tit in a brass bra but that was exactly the kind of weather he needed to slap some sense into him.

Maybe if he asked West nicely his cousin would punch him right in the face.

Chapter Six

S HANE WAITED UNTIL the waitress had poured them two coffees and hurried away before he spoke.

"Arden visited me tonight. She wants me to help find her father."

West shook his head and sighed. "I know she's angry with me but my hands are tied. He left a note and he's only been gone a day. Truthfully, I've already done too much."

"Did you find anything?"

West tapped his fingers on the edge of his coffee cup. "The cab company says they never picked him up, which leads us to believe someone else did. That someone may or may not have been the same person that drove Arden off the road. We didn't get anything at the traffic light, which means they went the other direction toward the highway instead of town."

That made sense if Ben was taking a road trip somewhere.

"Did you run his credit cards?"

"Now that's the interesting thing." West sat back in the booth. "He hasn't used them. His last transaction was lunch the day of the party, and that is strange. When you look at his transaction history he doesn't appear to use much cash."

"Any large withdrawals?"

"Nothing that made the police look twice, although they didn't look closely. I told them not to spend too much time on this."

Shane rubbed the back of his neck in frustration. "Have you analyzed his spending?"

West laughed and shook his head. "Hell, no. The police isn't even supposed to be working on this case, remember? But it sounds like you're going to."

"I'm a fucking idiot but I said I would help her. I was thinking of calling Jason and getting a full background on Ben. It might tell me where he might have run off to so suddenly."

"Why don't you just hire Jason to do the digging for you?"

"I thought about that but they don't really do private investigation work. They're police consultants, right? I don't mind asking for a dossier on Cavendish but I'm hesitant to ask for a field agent too."

"I'm sure Jason would help you if you asked."

West could barely look Shane in the eye and it was getting annoying. "If you've got something to say, cousin, just spit it out."

"Do you think this is a good idea?"

Shane started laughing so hard a few heads whipped around at the other tables. "I certainly do not but I couldn't say no." He immediately sobered as an image of Arden's worried face appeared before him. "She's terrified for him, West. Now that she knows what her father has done and the company he keeps, she's afraid something bad has happened to him. Frankly, I don't blame her, although I'm not convinced that he's anywhere against his will."

West leaned forward, his expression strained. "Mark my words, Shane. Nothing good can come from this. Either you find out he's playing roulette and drinking scotch in Vegas or even worse, you find out he's gotten in with some bad dudes that don't play. It won't end well for anyone, and Ben sure as hell isn't going to change his mind about you. He'd never bless a union between you and Arden."

Shane sucked in a sharp breath. "There isn't going to be any union. That's all in the past."

"You're just helping her as one fellow Tremont resident to the other, I suppose," West jeered with a grin. "Don't bullshit a bullshitter. You're still in love with her."

Done. Shane was done with this conversation. All of it. He stood and threw down some bills to cover the coffee. "Thanks for your help. I'll take it from here."

West was up and out of the booth before Shane could move past him. "Hey, I didn't mean to piss you off. I'm just saying that you need to be honest with yourself as to why you're doing this or you're going to end up in a world of hurt when this is all over. I hate to see that happen to you, man."

Shane simply shrugged into his coat and palmed his keys.

"I'm already in hell, West. This isn't going to make any difference."

✦　✦　✦

THE NEXT EVENING, Arden shouldn't have been surprised by Shane standing at her door holding a brown paper bag but she was. Somewhere in her over-emotional brain she'd fooled herself into thinking that him helping her wouldn't mean they'd be thrown together in close proximity.

Stupid. Stupid. Stupid.

"We need to talk," he stated, holding up the bag. Mouth-watering aromas wafted from its contents and her stomach growled in response. "I brought dinner. We have a lot of work to get through."

Stepping back to let him enter, her hand automatically shot up to smooth her still damp curls. She'd showered after school but hadn't bothered to do her hair or put on any makeup.

"What did you bring to eat?"

Shane smiled over his shoulder as he headed straight for the kitchen. "All your favorites. I know you love breakfast for dinner. Pancakes, biscuits with some fresh honey, hash browns, and of course, bacon."

She was practically drooling. The years had added a few pounds here and there and she had to watch her figure now, unlike the young girl she'd once been. She had a vivid memory of the two of them demolishing an order of chili cheese fries right before eating the largest hot fudge sundae she'd ever seen.

She closed the front door and trailed after him. "I'll get fat."

He emptied the bag while she pulled plates and silverware from cabinets and drawers. "I doubt you'll get fat from one hearty breakfast."

"I don't burn calories like I used to."

Stealing glances at him, Arden poured two glasses of water before settling in at the table. He was dressed casually today in jeans and a long-sleeved t-shirt that showed off why women in six counties couldn't keep their panties on when he turned on the charm.

She'd been one of them once.

"No one does, princess. It's all part of the aging process."

Shane sat across from her and dug into his food, paying little attention to her, which was fine. He'd filled her plate and she found herself eating most of it, her appetite sharp despite all the turmoil she'd been through in the last twenty-four hours. She'd thought the silence would be filled with tension but it was surprisingly comfortable. This wasn't the first meal they'd shared and Shane had never been much of a talker when he was filling his belly.

When she couldn't eat another bite, she set her fork down on the plate. "What do you want to talk about? Have you learned anything about where Dad went?"

"No, but I've got Jason and his men doing some digging into your father's business dealings." Shane pushed his plate away and wrapped his hands around his glass. "If we have any hope at all of making this partnership of sorts work then we need to set down some ground rules. Otherwise one or both of us are going to end up saying something we regret. I don't want to argue with you about the past."

"What kind of ground rules did you have in mind?"

"We leave the past where it is and start fresh. Try to be friends or at least two people who don't hate each other."

It sounded tempting and too good to be true. She didn't want them to have that kind of animosity between them.

"You won't bring up that summer?"

His eyebrows lifted and the corner of his lips turned up in a smile. "What summer?"

Smirking asshole.

"And this is a peace treaty?" she pressed. "No throwing the past in my face?"

"Not now." He leaned forward in his chair and she caught a whiff of his body wash mixed with his own masculine scent. Her bare toes curled against the cold tile as a shiver ran down her spine. "But after we find your father it will be a different story. We'll have it out then and I'll want the truth, Arden. You owe me an explanation as to why you left without a word and I think it's time you gave it to me. Until then though we're the best of friends. Deal?"

She did owe him. Dammit.

"Deal. When does this friendship start?"

"Why, it already has, princess. I brought you breakfast, didn't I?"

"I suppose I'm doing the dishes?"

She was pleased and surprised that she managed to keep her tone light-hearted.

"I think it's only fair." He stood and refilled his glass, leaning a hip against the counter. "Now let's get down to business, shall we? I need to know everything you know about your dad's life. No detail is too small or too off the wall. Anything might tell us where he might have gone."

She opened her mouth to answer but then closed it, realizing she didn't know all that much about her own father. He'd made a point not to expose her to his business dealings and only superficially to his personal relationships.

"I don't know much."

"You know more than you think you do. Let's start with recent events. Tell me anyone you know he's talked to since you've been home, whether on the phone or in person." Shane dug his cell out of his pocket and pressed a few buttons before laying it on the table. "If you don't mind I'll record this."

Arden had been home less than a month so this first exercise wasn't too bad. "On my first day home, he was in the office with Sheldon Court. I think he's in construction or something but I don't know what they were talking about. He stayed for about an hour and then left."

"Good girl. This is exactly what I need. Keep going."

She shouldn't have this warm feeling inside from simply being praised but then it had always been like that. She'd glowed under his approval, blossoming under his tender loving care and attention.

She couldn't help the small pinch of longing to feel that way again.

Chapter Seven

B Y THURSDAY NIGHT, Arden was exhausted and more worried than ever. She hadn't heard a word from her father and according to the police he hadn't used any of his credit cards or his cell phone. Every passing day with the same deafening silence only made things worse.

So she'd been thrilled when Shane told her he had the background check from Jason's firm. It felt like they were spinning their wheels with no new information and her nerves were stretched thin. She wanted something – anything – to happen.

Which was why she was knocking on his front door after school was done for the day. She'd been waiting since lunch time when she'd seen his text and patience had never been her strong suit.

The door swung open and Shane stood on the other side looking too handsome for words. They'd spent every single evening together this week going over the smallest of details she could remember about her father, so she ought to be used to how sexy and masculine he looked. He'd matured into a gorgeous man.

A nice one too.

Once they'd put aside the past and decided to be friends their time together had been rather easy and jovial. His sense of humor was still as wicked, and coupled with his keen intelligence he could make her laugh at will.

"Come on in. You look cold."

"That's because I am cold. It's freezing out there today. I'd forgotten how early it gets cold here at home."

Toeing off her boots, she hung her coat on the peg next to the door before joining him in front of the fireplace.

"Are you hungry?"

Shaking her head, she held her frozen hands closer to the flames, sighing as the heat penetrated her cold bones. "Not right now. Honestly I want to hear what they dug up."

Shane's expression had been bland so far, giving away nothing, but then he would have been an excellent poker player.

The asshole.

"Can I get you a drink?"

He'd tipped his hand just a little.

"You said we needed to meet but you don't seem to want to talk. Shane, that worries me."

He picked up a folder from the coffee table and sat down on the couch. "I know that you and I have been talking about your father all week, and I know that you are aware that your father's business dealings are at best unethical and at worst possibly illegal. I assume you've made your peace with that."

If he thought he was going to shock her with a story about bribes or under the table deals he was sadly mistaken. "I have, and for all he's done he is still my father. I can love him for how he took care of me after my mother died but not condone the way he has lived his life otherwise. You're not going to send me into a fainting spell. I know what my father is, Shane."

He opened the file and laid it flat on the table, his fingertips making circles on the pages, and his gaze deliberately averted. Finally, he looked her in the eye and picked up a photo, handing it to her.

"Do you know who this is? Does he look familiar?"

It was a picture of her father but...not her father. This man was a few pounds heavier with more gray hair.

"I don't understand. Who is this?"

She studied the picture, trying to see all the differences between this man and Ben Cavendish and ended up seeing all the similarities.

"It's your father's brother, David Hollis. Are you sure you've never seen him before?"

Frowning, she shook her head in confusion. "My father doesn't have a brother. He was an orphan. His parents were killed by a drunk driver and he lived in and out of foster homes until he was eighteen."

The man did *look* like Ben Cavendish, but they say that everyone has a twin somewhere.

Shane snorted but didn't laugh. Clearly, what he had to say he didn't think was funny. "Of course he'd tell you some heroic tale of pulling himself up by his bootstraps. Your father does have a brother though. He came from a rather wealthy family actually and went to the best schools. His parents did pass away but from cancer and heart disease, and only after he was an adult."

Arden's hand shook as she looked at the photo again. "I really have an uncle? Relatives?"

Her entire life she'd been brought up to believe she and her father and grandmother were alone in the world. Raising her gaze back to Shane, she could see the battle he was fighting within himself. There was more and she wasn't going to like it. Setting the photo back down, she took a deep breath to slow her racing heart.

"I have a feeling that old saying about the truth hurting is going to apply, isn't it? The best way to remove a bandage is to rip it off, so you might as well just spill it. I can take it. I promise."

His brows were pulled down with concern and she almost reached up to smooth away the lines in his forehead. "You need to sit down. It's a long story, honey."

Arden sank into the cushions on the couch next to Shane, needing his strength at this moment and suddenly exceedingly glad that he'd promised to be her friend. She had a feeling she was going to need one before this day was over.

✦ ✦ ✦

IF SHANE HAD had any idea what Jason's team was going to dig up he never would have agreed to help Arden. After reading the information, Shane had wanted to punch Ben Cavendish right in the mouth. He'd lied to his daughter for so long and about so many things, Shane doubted the man knew what the truth was anymore, if he ever had. Honesty had never been a hallmark of Cavendish's business ventures.

"Let's start with your name." Shane cleared his throat, unsure as to how he should proceed. He wished he didn't care quite so much right about now. "Ben was born Benjamin Hollis in Hemingdale, Indiana. He legally changed it later when he moved to Tremont. I think you would have been about eighteen months old."

He watched as she took in the tidbit of information, obviously curious as to what it meant. He'd started here because where the story truly began was going to cause tears and heartache.

"Hollis." She seemed to be trying the name out for size. "Okay, he changed his name and didn't tell me about his family. Is he an outcast? Did they disown him?"

His sweet Arden. She was desperately trying to make her father some kind of hero in this scenario and in a way he probably was. Although he'd lied to his only daughter, he'd never shirked from his duties as a parent.

"They didn't disown him. He left after your mother died."

Another frown. "Mother died here in Tremont. Her grave is in the church cemetery."

Shit, Shane hated what he had to do.

"Your mother's grave is in Hemingdale, a little town just outside of Indianapolis." He pulled the death certificate from the file and held it out to her. "From what they could find out, your father paid for an empty grave in the local cemetery for the woman that you would know as Susannah Cavendish, but she died with the name Susannah Hollis."

Her shaking fingers pushed back her curls from her face and he couldn't stop himself from capturing that hand and holding it in his. The least he could do was be there for her because she sure as hell was going to need someone by the time he was done.

She squeezed his hand as if in thanks. "Holy hell, he went to all that trouble? He created a fake grave? What the hell is wrong with him? Why didn't he tell me the truth?"

"Probably because the truth was ugly." The discarded death certificate sat on her thigh and he reached for it, bracing himself for her reaction. "You told me your mother died of leukemia but that's not what the investigation showed. According to the newspaper reports and the death certificate, your mother was shot in her own home."

Chapter Eight

THE ROOM SEEMED to fall away and Shane's voice echoed in her ears as Arden struggled to make sense of his words. Her body and mind went completely numb to keep her emotions in check. She couldn't afford to break down until she knew it all.

"Shot? She had cancer."

Shane's thumb caressed the pulse point at her wrist but the action barely registered. "She was shot, honey. I'm so very sorry to have to tell you all this. We can stop here if we need to."

"No." Arden shook her head and pulled her hand away from Shane, wringing them together. "Keep going. All of it, please."

Shane exhaled slowly but didn't argue, for which she was grateful. "They never found the person who did it apparently, and there wasn't much evidence and no witnesses to the actual crime."

I've been lied to my entire life.

"Where was Daddy?"

"Your father was on a business trip in St. Louis." Shane paused, waiting for her to speak but she didn't have anything to say. She didn't even know how to feel yet. "From what Jason's firm was able to dig up your father decided to give you a new life, so he changed his name and moved both of you to Tremont where he started a business here. Your grandmother must have missed you because she followed six months later. Your mother did have a best friend who still lives there, although no other family."

"I could use a drink."

She could use several but she'd start with one and go from there. Shane stood and disappeared into the kitchen before returning with a highball glass and a bottle. He sat the glass down on the coffee table and front of her and filled it halfway with an amber liquid.

"Whiskey. Sip it, honey, don't gulp."

Wrapping her cold, shaking fingers around the cut crystal, she took a swallow and closed her eyes as the alcohol burned all the way down into her stomach. The pain was exactly what she needed to jolt her out of her emotionless state. Tears of anger and hurt began to well up and she rubbed at her eyes to keep them from falling.

"Is there anymore?"

"We weren't able to get many details on the shooting other than what was in the newspapers at the time. Jason's friend Jared is still digging but I'm not sure he'll find much more."

More sips of the whiskey and more heat sliding down her abdomen. She wasn't much of a drinker, so the liquor would go straight to her head if she wasn't careful. The last thing she needed to do was get drunk in front of Shane.

"There's more about your father though."

She held the glass with both hands to keep them from shaking. "Of course there is. Let me guess, he works for MI-6 and he's licensed to kill by the Queen of England."

"He's broke."

Arden jerked her gaze away from the floor to look into Shane's eyes. "That's not possible. My father is a successful businessman. Look at his house. His cars. He travels by private jet. He can't be broke."

Shane pulled a few pieces of paper from the file and held them up for her but she didn't reach out for them, content to keep a hold of the highball glass like a lifeline. When she didn't take them, he sighed and set them back down on the table.

"Honey, from what they were able to find your father has always lived on the edge. He's taken big chances in business and leveraged the hell out of himself. That's great if you win, but if you don't it can wipe you out. The economic downturn in 2008 hit everyone hard and your father wasn't immune. He lost pretty much everything and has been holding on by a thread. He has assets but he also owes a lot of money."

Arden knocked back the rest of her drink and reached for the bottle to refill that glass but Shane's hand stayed her movement.

"I'm a grown woman."

"Unless you've changed, you're also a lightweight who could get tipsy on one glass of wine. You always were a cheap date."

Reluctantly she placed the glass on the table. She hated it but he was right. "Do you think that's why my father disappeared? That it has something to do with his finances?"

"I'd say that's the best guess at this time. We only know what he owes through legitimate sources. He might have borrowed money under the table from some less than ethical people."

This evening was getting better and better. All she needed

was some pestilence and plague to make everything perfect. "You're saying he's hiding out. That they might want him dead."

Shane's warm, strong arms slid around her, pulling her next to him as a finger tipped up her chin so she was looking into his eyes. At first she struggled; it had been so long since she'd been held with such tenderness. She and Michael's physical relationship had ended long before the separation and divorce. But Shane's implacable hold didn't allow any protest and she settled back against the cushions and let herself luxuriate in someone else being strong.

But just for a moment. That's all she would allow.

"You knew this was a possibility. You said you were aware of Ben's actions."

"Not specific incidents but I had a pretty good idea. Still, it's one thing to know them and another to realize that he might have to face the consequences of those decisions. I'm even more worried now, Shane. He could be in real danger."

Shane's lips were pressed together and his brows pulled down. "I hate to break this to you but you could be too. If he owes money to the wrong people they might figure that you are Ben's one weakness and he'd do anything to keep you safe."

It was all too much and her mind and body rebelled. The whiskey and her lunch suddenly pushed into her throat and she was up and off the couch, bolting for the powder room off the foyer. Kneeling in front of the toilet, she emptied the contents of her stomach as strong, soothing hands lifted her hair out of the way and stroked her back.

With hot tears rolling down her cheeks, she slumped against the vanity while Shane flushed and then wet a cloth with warm water. He bathed the cold sweat from her neck and face before tossing it into the sink and scooping her into his arms and laying her gently on the couch.

"Stay here. I'll get you some ginger ale for your stomach."

Where was she going to go? Her legs were too weak to take her anywhere and besides, everything she thought was true about her life was a total lie. She didn't even know where to begin to make any sense out of it.

And now she might be a target.

Shane came back into the living room and placed a tumbler in her hands, wrapping his own around hers to steady them. "Here you go. Just sip it and see if it will stay down."

With his help, she took a small drink and then a few more, clearing the sour taste from her mouth. "Thank you for taking care of me. You didn't have to."

Smoothing her curls back, he gave her a gentle smile. "That's what friends do."

She placed her palm over her aching heart and rubbed at the spot, trying to ease the pain that was currently in residence. "I'm glad I'm your friend."

"We'll figure this out. I'm going to find your father and I'm not going to let anything happen to you."

"I know."

She did know. Even if he hated her guts he wouldn't let anything hurt her. That's the kind of man he was and always had been. She'd spent her entire adult life comparing other men to Shane and he'd always been head and shoulders above anyone else. He probably always would be.

"You're going to be okay, honey. You can handle this."

But it felt good not to have to handle it alone.

✦   ✦   ✦

ARDEN HAD FALLEN asleep on the couch, worn out emotionally and physically after being sick and having a good cry. Shane had felt like ten kinds of shit telling her about the contents of the file, but there was really no good way to tell someone they'd been lied to all their life. He'd carried her into his bedroom and laid her on the mattress, covering her with a light blanket.

With her head on his pillow, she looked like she belonged in his bed.

He'd better not get any fantasies or funny ideas just because she showed a little weakness and let him cuddle her for a few minutes. She'd wake rested and ready to be prickly as hell again and he might as well make peace with that. She wasn't going to suddenly turn to him and say she'd made a mistake all those years ago when she left. He wasn't one of her regrets.

Now he was sitting at the kitchen table with Wyatt Stone who had agreed to help Shane look for Ben Cavendish. The man worked for Jason's law enforcement consulting business but he had a real knack for finding people that didn't want to be found. Not long before, he'd found a fugitive that had tried to frame a friend of Travis's for murder.

"We don't have much to go on," Shane admitted. "He's not using his credit cards and we have no idea even which direction he may have gone. We don't even know why he left. I only have suspicions."

Wyatt scratched his chin as he leafed through the file. At six-foot-three inches and two hundred and thirty pounds, he was a big man that made the chair he was sitting in look tiny. As powerfully built as he was, Stone had a gentle manner about him that was quiet and unassuming. It was an excellent combination for getting people to talk – intimidating and caring all at the same time.

"If he's on the run I'm guessing he would go somewhere familiar, someplace he's been before and felt comfortable. I'll look at his travel history and see what I can find." Wyatt looked up from the papers. "What's your gut telling you?"

Shane chuckled at the bald query. "I'm not a cop so I don't think my gut instinct counts. But if you're asking then I'll say that Ben Cavendish is a total asshole who has never been afraid of pissing off anyone. At least not that I've been aware of. So running away doesn't seem in character for him. But he isn't a man that is filled with courage either. He gets other people to get their hands dirty instead of him. He likes to stay separate from the little people."

"Little people? Who is he? Napoleon?"

Memories of the day Ben had told him Arden left for the East Coast filled Shane's mind like it was yesterday. The older man had been so triumphant, so fucking smug while Shane had been filled with anger and a sense of helplessness. The bastard had clearly enjoyed the hands-on delivery of that message. It still filled Shane with rage all these years later.

"Not a bad comparison, actually. Ben loves the trappings of success. He likes to feel special and he loves people to cater to him. How Arden turned out so normal I'll never know. It was probably the influence of her grandmother. They have a close relationship."

It hadn't escaped Shane's notice that Elaine Graham would have had to know all about her daughter's murder and Ben's changing his name. Arden hadn't put that part of the puzzle together yet but she soon would, and she was going to be hurt and probably pretty pissed about it. She trusted her grandmother implicitly even when she didn't trust Ben.

"Do you think she's in danger?"

Shane shrugged helplessly, still trying to wrap his mind around what he'd learned. "I just don't know. Part of me wants to wrap her in cotton wool and keep an eye on her and the other part knows that will only make her mad and frustrated. I need to find some happy medium where I'm assured that she's safe but she has her freedom too."

"You could get Jason to put a tail on her," Wyatt suggested with a gleam of mischief in his eye. "She'd never have to know."

"I'm tempted," Shane admitted with a groan. "But if she finds out my testicles will be in a jar on the mantle. She may not look it but she's got a temper, my friend."

"Afraid of a bitty thing like her? I think you can take her, Shane."

"She fights dirty," Shane retorted. "Now where do we stand? Do you have enough to get started on? I wish I had more."

Wyatt laughed and stood tucking his notes into his pocket and pulling on his coat. "I've started with less so this isn't actually that bad. I'll check into his known haunts and with his friends, discreetly of course. I've got a friend at TSA that might be able to help us out as well if Cavendish flew under an assumed name. We'll find him. If his habits are as expensive as you make out, he'll have to surface eventually. In the meantime, take care of your woman. She's got a lot to deal with."

"She's not my woman," Shane replied automatically. "Not even close."

Chuckling and shaking his head, Wyatt slapped Shane on the back. "I've spent my life studying human nature and let me tell you something. You've got the look of a man in love. If she's not yours then you need to do something to fix that situation as soon as possible."

Christ, did it show that clearly? Did Arden see it too?

"This isn't something I can fix," Shane said simply. "This goes back a long time. We're just friends now. I was the only one she could come to for help."

Wyatt gave him a shrewd look. "Could come to or wanted to come to? I'm not telling you your business, Shane, but take it from someone who knows what they're talking about. The past can be an anchor if you let it. Shake it off, man. If you love her don't let anything stand in your way. Go all out. If I were in your shoes that's what I'd do."

Wyatt left and Shane padded softly into his bedroom to check on Arden, who was still sleeping peacefully. Relaxed and serene, he listened to the sounds of her breathing and watched the rise and fall of her chest, his fingers gripping the molding on the door until his knuckles were white.

He simply wasn't sure he was strong enough to go there. If she walked away again…hell, he'd barely survived the heartache last time. Round two would be even more painful and devastating.

The fact was he'd never been as happy in his life as he was that summer with this woman. He'd pretended that everything was great but deep inside he'd missed her more than he could articulate. Now he'd agreed to help her because, let's face it, he was weak and wanted to be with her even though he knew it was stupid as shit to see her and spend time with her. He was dumb as a bag of doorknobs.

He'd never stopped loving Arden.

Chapter Nine

A RDEN WAS MAKING herself crazy. One second she hated her father and then the next she wanted to hug him after all he'd been through. Clearly he'd been trying to protect her from growing up as the "girl whose mother had been shot" and that was admirable, but he should have told her the truth when she became an adult. As it was, she had so many questions and there was only one way to get the answers.

After her last class on Friday, she'd stopped into the principal's office for a chat. Keith Centers was a good man and admitted he'd heard that her father had left town under somewhat mysterious circumstances. When she filled in few details he was more than willing to give her what she asked for. Time off. She was only a substitute, after all.

Dammit, she hated herself for asking. She'd wanted this job and now a month into the school year she was asking for a leave of absence, but this was important. If she was fired, so be it. Finding her father and learning about all that had been kept secret from her had to take priority over everything else in her life.

Back in her classroom, Arden cleaned the dry erase board

and straightened up the room before leaving. She was finishing up the last of her work when a noise made her look up.

"I've been standing here awhile." Shane stood in the doorway looking like he'd spent the day on the ranch. "You were completely engrossed in your writing."

Quickly emailing the notes to Keith, she closed the laptop with a loud click. "I was making assignment notes for the new substitute next week."

Shane took off his hat and tossed it onto a desk. "*New* substitute? Are you sick?"

Arden didn't have to have spent the last fifteen years with Shane to know how this conversation was going to go. He wasn't going to stop her but he was going to try.

She began packing away her papers and books into her messenger bag. "No, I'm not sick. I'm going to meet my family that I've never met and find out about my mother's murder."

She was also going to have a long talk with her grandmother when she came back, but not before. Elaine wasn't going to be allowed to make excuses for what she'd done and then try and talk Arden out of this trip. Angry with her grandmother for lying all these years, Arden wasn't ready to face her yet without losing her temper.

"I had a feeling you'd say that." Shane squeezed himself into one of the desks, dwarfing it with his large frame. "That's why I made arrangements for someone to cover my office next week. We leave as soon as you can get packed."

Mouth hanging open, Arden couldn't believe her ears. "You're not going to try and stop me? Talk me out of it?"

Chuckling, Shane stretched out his long legs. "Doubt it

would do any good so I might as well just go with it. You've found out some very disturbing things and it's only normal that you'd want to check all this out for yourself. I'm going to help you."

Arden fell back into her chair, still not believing her ears. "I thought you'd try and stop me. I thought you'd tell me all the reasons I shouldn't go."

"Seems to me the only reason would be that you might lose your job by taking time off so early, and I don't think that would compel you to stay." He grinned, showing off the Anderson dimple in his cheek and looking so darn smug she wanted to kick his shin. "It would appear, princess, that you've forgotten quite a bit these last few years, especially about how I indulge your every whim. When have I ever been able to say no to you unless it involved your health and safety?"

Searching the nooks and crannies of her mind, she was surprised that she couldn't think of one time that he had. He only put up barriers when he thought something might be dangerous or unhealthy, like the time she wanted to bungee off a bridge with a few of her friends. He'd been right of course, as they really didn't know what they were doing and would have managed to get them all killed if he hadn't talked some sense into them.

"You're going with me?"

It shouldn't make her happy but a thrill shot through her body. This friendship stuff was not too bad. She could get used to this.

"I certainly cannot let you go alone. Ben is still missing and we don't know why. Until then, I think it's prudent for someone to keep an eye on you and that someone is me. Are you okay with that?"

Her brain said no but her heart screamed yes a helluva lot louder. As painful as it was being with him, she learned it was even harder when she wasn't.

"I'm fine with it, but don't you have a business to run?"

"A good executive makes sure the people who work for him are smarter than he is. The company will be fine and they can reach me by phone if they need me. So I'll pick you up at the house in an hour? Can you be ready?"

She opened her mouth to ask all sorts of questions about the travel arrangements he'd made but changed her mind. The fact was she trusted him to take care of it. He might have been a womanizing playboy but he'd also been organized and on the ball. All she needed to do was sit back and enjoy the journey.

"I can, friend. Thank you for everything."

He ran his finger around his collar as if he was embarrassed. "We'll figure out this friendship thing. In the meantime, we have a plane to catch."

"I meant what I said. Thank you, Shane. You didn't have to do this or any of it. You're helping me because I begged you to when I'm sure you'd rather be doing eight hundred other things, but please believe me when I tell you that I am grateful. I know I couldn't do this without you."

She hoped he could hear the sincerity in her voice. No matter what she'd said to him in the past, she was truly appreciative of what he was doing for her.

"I think you could do anything you set your mind to."

She watched his retreating figure, listening to the echo of his boots on the tile floor. She'd always wanted to believe what he said but she knew better. There was one thing she could never do.

Make Shane fall in love with her again.

✦ ✦ ✦

AFTER A SMOOTH takeoff, Shane unbuckled his seatbelt and sat his briefcase on the table in front of him. They had an almost three hour flight ahead of them to Indianapolis so he might as well take the opportunity to get some paperwork done and out of the way.

The smiling air hostess stood next to his seat and leaned down, showing off a bit of cleavage. She was a lovely woman with straight brown hair and blue eyes along with a nice figure, but what she didn't understand was that no one could hold a candle to Arden Cavendish. When she was in the room, every other female ceased to exist.

"Anything else I can get you, Shane? Coffee? Tea? Maybe another whiskey?"

Shane lifted the half-full highball glass. "This should do it for now. Thank you, Sherry. Arden, is there anything you'd like besides your water?"

Looking up from her magazine, she shook her head. "I'm fine, thank you."

"Then that's it. We'll call you if we need anything."

He didn't think he imagined Sherry's look of disappointment as she left the main cabin. He'd never given her much, if any, encouragement but the mirthful expression on Arden's face said she thought the opposite.

Shane rolled his eyes and took another sip of his whiskey.

"What?"

Peeping over the top of her magazine, Arden's lips were pressed together in what appeared to be an effort to keep from laughing. "Nothing. Nothing at all. Do your paperwork or whatever it is that millionaire tycoons do on their corporate jet."

"Stop acting like you've never flown in a private plane. I know better."

She didn't answer, going back to reading her magazine. Shane tried to concentrate on the contracts in front of him but he felt a pair of blue eyes gazing at him. Finally he slapped the papers down on the table with a growl.

"What?" he asked again, intending to get an answer this time.

"You," she replied with a barely suppressed laugh. "This important businessman is a far cry from the boy in cutoff jeans and torn t-shirts I used to know. You even have the flight attendants flirting with you. Are you and she…"

"No, we are not. And as for how I look, I suppose we've both grown up and changed but I do still have t-shirts and cutoffs. I only wear them on the weekends now or when I'm doing yard work."

Arden's gaze lingered on the door Sherry had exited through. "You always did have women panting after you. Even for an Anderson, you overachieved in that category."

A small bit of hope began to unfurl in his abdomen. It sounded like Arden was jealous. Maybe just a little bit.

"I do not have women panting after me. And as for Sherry she was just being polite and helpful. Getting us food and drink is part of her job description."

Arden closed the magazine and shook her head. "She bent down so you could get a good look at her chest and maybe her bra."

Black lace. Probably a front-closure but he'd been fooled before.

"I'm not interested," he stated flatly because it was the God's honest truth. Not even if Arden hadn't been there would Shane have taken Sherry up on her offer. He didn't mix business with pleasure and she was an employee of Anderson Industries.

"She's very beautiful. And tall."

Chuckling, Shane shoved his paperwork into his briefcase. "You think everyone is tall."

"Compared to me everyone is." She played with her water bottle. "So what's the plan when we get to Indianapolis?"

He tucked his case away and reached for his highball glass. "We'll get a hotel for the night and then in the morning we'll rent a car and drive to Hemingdale. Once we get there, I thought you might want to visit your mother's grave first thing."

Arden gave him a misty smile. "That's thoughtful of you. I'd like that."

His heart lurched in his chest but pointedly ignored it. "It's all part of our new friendship."

"Then you're a good friend."

If she called him the brother she'd never had he'd jump from the plane without a parachute.

"After that, I thought we'd try and see your mother's best friend. I'm sure she has a lot of information that wasn't in any file."

Arden slowly stood and walked up and down the aisle a few

times. Shane didn't say anything, content to let her work out whatever it was she needed to. Eventually, she sat back down and gripped the leather covered arms of her seat. "What if I find out something truly horrible? I mean, something even worse than my mother being shot? If Dad went to all that trouble to protect me then the truth could be totally devastating."

"That certainly did occur to me," Shane conceded. "Do you want me to have the pilot turn the plane around? I can do that if you're scared."

Her face flamed with outrage. "I'm not scared."

He didn't mind admitting to himself he liked to push Arden a little. Every now and then he'd see flashes of the spirited girl he'd known, but too often she was quiet and subdued. He wanted to see the fire and passion that had made her the most exciting woman he'd ever known.

"If you say so."

Arden leaned forward, her eyes narrowing. "I do say so. I'm not afraid."

"You said that. Do you want me to turn the plane around or not? We can be back in Montana in a few hours."

Hopping up from the chair, she turned her back to him, her arms crossed over her chest.

"You are such a jerk, Shane Anderson. I do not want to turn around and I am not scared."

"Being afraid isn't a bad thing, honey. This is an unusual situation and there is a high probability that you're going to learn things about your family's past that you aren't going to like. You wouldn't be human if you didn't have some trepidation."

She whirled around to face him. "Trepidation, yes. Fear, no."

His mouth slowly turned up at the corners. She was damn beautiful when she had a head of steam going.

"I stand corrected."

She fell back into the seat, one leg crossed over the other, tugging down the waistband of her jeans and exposing a strip of creamy skin on her belly. "I can see right through you, you know. You did that on purpose."

He hadn't been trying to hide it but if he wanted to he could have. Quite well, as a matter of fact.

"Yes, but look at you now. Your eyes are sparkling, your skin has flushed pink, and you're more alive than you've been since the night of the party. When I first saw you that night I thought I might have to give you CPR. You've been walking through your days half-alive."

Her smile faded and her gaze dropped to the table between them. "Growing older can be hard on a person. Not all of us live a charmed life, Shane."

Never in his wildest dreams had he thought of his life as charmed, although he knew he was a lucky son of a bitch to have been born into the Anderson family. Not just because of the wealth but because they were people who truly knew how to love.

"Maybe you'll tell me about the last several years sometime."

She lifted her eyes to his, her forehead wrinkled in confusion. "You want to hear about...my marriage...my life? Why?"

Because he was an idiot who couldn't get enough of her even if it broke his own heart into thousands of pieces.

"Because I care," he answered simply. "Because talking about it might help. I'm your friend, remember?"

It was better than not having her in his life at all.

She didn't answer for a long moment. "I doubt you'd be interested but thank you for the offer. I think I'm going to close my eyes and try to take a little nap before we get there. It's been a long day."

Shane nodded and Arden reclined the seat and closed her eyes. He ought to do the same but his mind was whirling at a hundred miles per hour. Thoughts of the past and the present collided and visions of the future made his chest hurt. He wasn't what she wanted and he couldn't even be a listening board for her. Reminding himself once again that she'd left him, he picked up the newspaper from a side table and began to sightlessly page through it. This trip wasn't going to be some kind of fairy tale where she miraculously changed her mind and declared her undying love and devotion.

That only happened in movies.

Chapter Ten

I T WAS LATE when they arrived at the hotel in Indianapolis. Arden yawned as Shane paid the taxi driver and picked up their bags. She'd given him a token protest but he simply walked by her to the front desk as if she hadn't spoken. Trailing after him, she couldn't help but admire his wide shoulders and powerful arms that so effortlessly carried their suitcases.

Within minutes, they had checked in and opened the door to a lovely suite on one of the upper floors. Shane dropped the luggage off to the side and shrugged off his jacket while her eyes zeroed in on the bed. One bed. Her expression must have given her away because he rolled his eyes and walked over to the large windows that overlooked the city.

"Relax. There's another bed in the loft up there." Shane pointed to the top of a stairway tucked into the corner of the room. "Do you want to sleep up there or down here? I'm beat and ready to hit the sack."

Arden attempted to act nonchalant, leaning against the bar. "Of course there is. I knew that."

He was openly laughing at her and she didn't think her next action completely through. Pulling her paperback from her purse, she launched it at his head. His quick reflexes allowed him to easily duck the projectile and it fell harmlessly to the floor after hitting the wall and bouncing off.

She'd only made him grin wider and at that moment he looked so much like the young man she'd fallen in love with. Optimistic and fun, he had a smile that could light up a dark day.

"Now that's what I like to see, a little fire and spirit. I'll take the bed upstairs. There's a small bathroom up there as well so this one is all yours. Night, Arden."

Grabbing his suitcase, Shane took the stairs two at a time and disappeared up in the loft area. She stood there for a few moments and listened to the sounds he made – unzipping his suitcase, kicking off his shoes, and then the sound of water running in the shower.

Gulping, Arden quickly turned away and dragged her own bag over to the bed, determined not to think about Shane taking a shower.

Naked. Soapy.

She smacked her forehead and groaned, saying a silent curse that Shane Anderson still had the ability to get her all hot and bothered. She'd been married and yet here she was acting like a teenage virgin getting her first look at a man's bare body.

And what a body it was.

She remembered quite well how he'd looked like a Greek god then and probably ten times better now. He'd filled out some and the way his muscles moved and bunched under his shirt had her fanning her face. She was burning up at the mere thought of Shane taking a freaking shower. She'd passed sad and was all the way to pathetic. It would be even more humiliating if he ever found out how long it had been since she'd been intimate with a man or even worse, how many times she'd fantasized about him over the years.

Shaking her head in self-disgust, she retrieved her pajama shorts and a t-shirt from her suitcase and headed for the bathroom. Ten minutes later she was tucked up in bed, her teeth clean and her body exhausted. Up early for school this morning, she'd had a long day and despite everything she'd learned this week she easily fell asleep.

It was the thunder that woke her up a few hours later and she sat straight up in bed, the air knocked from her lungs. She reminded herself to breathe as she crawled across the mattress and reached over to the heavy drapes to tug them aside. A flash of jagged lightning lit the sky, blinding her for a moment and then another loud rumble of thunder had her scrambling back under the covers. She hated storms and had never been able to get used to the sound and fury.

"It's a real doozy, isn't it?" She hadn't heard Shane's soft footsteps come down the stairs, but he was suddenly standing right next to her bed wearing nothing but a pair of boxer shorts. Holy moly, did he look amazing. Time had not only been kind to Shane, it had been downright generous. He was gorgeous. "Are you okay, princess?"

The lightning illuminated his form, throwing shadows over the dips and planes of his muscular body. She sucked in oxygen as she shook her muddled head, trying to find the ability to form words and sentences. She was a complete mess and it wasn't just the storm that had put her in this state.

"I'm fine. I'm okay."

Her voice came out squeaky and she heard his snort of disbelief. "You're a terrible liar and always have been. Do you want me to turn the television on or something? It might drown out the thunder."

Obviously he remembered her fear of thunderstorms. They'd once been trapped in the Anderson horse barn for several hours while a storm howled outside. Shane had found a pleasurable way of distracting her but she couldn't allow that to happen tonight. Not that he'd want to. She'd seen the beauty on his arm the night of the charity party and Arden was well aware she couldn't begin to compete with a woman as sexy as that.

He didn't wait for her reply, reaching for the remote on the nightstand and pressing a few buttons. An old black and white movie came on and captured Arden's attention from the noises outside. *The Thin Man* was one of her favorite films and it was a perfect distraction.

"William Powell and Myrna Loy, huh?" Shane chuckled and set the remote back down on the table. "Good choice. Can I make her ladyship a cup of tea or get her a soda to enjoy while she watches?"

Grabbing a pillow and hugging it to her chest, Arden pulled her knees up and wrapped her arms around her legs. If Shane wanted to play the commoner to her royalty she was going to let him. "If there's a ginger ale in that mini-bar I'd love one."

The suite had a wet bar in one corner with a small refrigerator to the side that had been fully stocked, according to the woman at the front desk. Sitting back and watching the story unfold, she heard two cans pop open and then Shane rejoined her, sliding her soda on the table next to her.

"Here you go."

He headed toward the stairs, presumably to go back to bed and that little voice inside of her told her to keep quiet and let him go.

She didn't listen.

Arden hated storms and she didn't want to be alone. The fact was now that she was used to seeing Shane she liked having him around. She'd missed him, honestly. They'd been more than lovers, they'd been friends too. He could make her laugh and make her feel safe all at the same time. It had been a long time since she'd felt that way and she craved it whether it was right or not.

"You don't have to go upstairs. I mean, if you don't want to. You can watch the movie with me. I know you like this one."

His steps paused and she waited, holding her breath and questioning her own sanity. Being his friend – just his friend – was harder than she'd ever imagined it would be but she was determined to make it so.

"I guess I could watch it again, at least until the storm dies down."

For a moment she thought he was going to hop into bed with her and stretch his long frame out on the mattress, but instead he settled onto the loveseat and propped his bare feet on the coffee table. They sat in silence for a long time and Arden was surprised at how comfortable the entire situation felt. There was no awkwardness or wishing she was somewhere else. It was just her and Shane doing something they'd done dozens of times in the past.

"Another?"

A commercial was on and Shane was pointing to her now empty can of soda.

"No, if I drink any more I'll be up all night for a completely different reason."

He tossed both of their empties in the trash can and then came to stand by the bed. "I'm going to head up. Are you going to be okay if I do?"

The storm had died down and now there was just rain and wind against the windows. Her fingers played with the corner of the pillow as she fought down the urge to ask him all sorts of questions that were none of her business.

She wanted to know if he'd missed her.

If he ever thought about her.

But she didn't ask him any of those things. Instead she smiled up at him as if her heart wasn't twisted in her chest until she almost couldn't breathe.

"Thank you," she said simply. "It helped having you here."

He pulled the drapes closed again, shutting out the lights from the city below. "You should get some sleep. We have a big day tomorrow."

Tears pricked the back of her eyes and she dragged her gaze away so he wouldn't see. She could never let him know how he still affected her. And if she wasn't over him after all this time, he probably always would.

"Good night, Shane."

"Night, Arden. Call me if you need me."

She didn't hear his bare feet on the carpeted stairs but she knew that he was in the loft. His scent, clean and citrusy, was fading and she took in a lungful of air to try and hold on to it. She didn't have much left of him and this was one thing she could have and he'd never know.

Sliding down under the covers, Arden left the television on, its sound soothing to her overwrought nerves. Her lids fluttered closed and she let thoughts of meeting a family she'd never known lull her to sleep and crowd out visions of the man who slept so peacefully upstairs.

So close, but he might as well be on the other side of the planet.

✦   ✦   ✦

ARDEN WAS TRYING to fucking kill him.

Shane moved restlessly in bed, throwing the covers off of his overheated body. He was trying so hard to be just a friend to Arden but it wasn't easy. Even tonight, it had taken all the willpower he had not to slide in bed next to her and pull her into his arms. He wanted to protect her, care for her, and love her. He wanted to be the man she turned to when she needed…anything…everything. But that was never going to happen.

This was what he could have. He could be the friend that she desperately needed right now and help her through what was from all appearances going to be a rough ride. The visit tomorrow to the cemetery was going to be tough and he would have to find a way to be there for her without letting her know how much he still wanted her. That would be a burden she couldn't deal with right now, or ever really. She'd left him and she showed no signs of regret about that action.

She didn't love him anymore and this wasn't a Disney movie.

He needed to figure out how to help her without pouring out all the feelings and emotions he'd bottled up for so long. She wouldn't be interested and it would only make her feel guilty while making him look like a loser.

Making a silent vow to himself, he promised to keep his distance, if only for his own peace of mind.

And heart.

Chapter Eleven

ARDEN'S FINGERS TIGHTLY gripped Shane's bicep as they walked over the green lawns of the Hemingdale Memorial Gardens. They'd stopped at a flower shop after breakfast and picked up a small wreath of flowers to place on the grave, but now that they were almost there he could feel Arden's pace slowing markedly. She was biting her lip and her skin was quite pale with what was probably fear and maybe anger too. She had every right to be upset with her family. They'd kept important details about her life secret even when she became an adult and Shane was glad that he was here to help her get through what would be a difficult few days.

He stopped walking and captured her hand in his. "We don't have to do this if you've changed your mind."

"I haven't. It's just emotional." Her voice was thick with tears and Shane had to remind himself that his comfort wouldn't be welcome. He longed to pull her into his arms and stroke her hair but instead he patted her shoulder in what he hoped was a tender manner.

"I'll be right beside you."

They walked to the middle of the row and Arden knelt down

to trace the engraving on the marble stone. "Beloved wife and mother. I wish I remembered her, Shane. Father and Grandmother told me about her but how can I trust anything they've said now? Maybe every single thing they've said about her was a lie."

There were tears sliding down her cheeks and he knelt as well to help her secure the floral wreath into the earth, his fingers brushing her skin. "You'll have a chance to talk to her best friend. I imagine she knows a great deal about your mother. I bet you'll hear some great stories from when they were kids."

They both stood and Arden wrapped her arms around her torso as she sniffled. He dug a handkerchief out of his pocket and dabbed at her cheeks before pressing it into her hand.

"Thank you," she murmured. "I guess I should start carrying around tissues or something. I seem to be blubbering like a baby every other minute these days. I know tears make men uncomfortable, so I'm really sorry about this. I'm trying to get myself under control here."

"Who the hell told you that? Tears are fine. You cry all you want to and don't worry about me."

Had her husband told her that she shouldn't cry? Or maybe her asshole father? It sounded like something Ben Cavendish would say in that infuriating pompous tone he liked to use so he sounded superior.

Arden scrubbed at her face, a sob catching in her throat. "It feels like I've lost her all over again. Isn't that weird? Shouldn't I be over this by now? I mean, I never really knew her, after all. How can I mourn a stranger?"

"She's not a stranger. You see her every time you look in the mirror, honey. I've seen a picture of her and you look just like her."

The resemblance had been uncanny except that her mother's hair was a darker shade of blonde and slightly shorter.

"That doesn't mean I know her."

He couldn't take this bullshit any longer. If she didn't want him she could push him away but he simply couldn't stand to hear the pain in her voice any longer. He reached out and placed his hands on her arms, pulling her close. "I think it's actually normal that you're going through this right now. Finding out that your mother died a violent death and then that she's buried here. You want answers and we're going to get them for you."

"I am afraid, Shane." Her voice quivered and more tears fell down her face. "What if she's nothing like what Daddy told me? What if she's not a good person? If I look like her am I going to become like her?"

Crushing her small frame to his much bigger body, he rocked her in his arms and whispered soothing words in her ear. She shook with sobs for a long time and then finally quieted, her head lying on his chest. He didn't stop himself from stroking her golden curls and then down her spine before wiping her damp cheeks. "You are not a bad person and I'd lay odds your mother wasn't either. But even if she was that doesn't mean you're going to be just like her. I look like my dad but he and I are very different people."

She gave him a watery smile. "You both like to fish and eat super hot wings."

"But he likes Hemingway and I prefer Fitzgerald. We have things in common but we're not exactly the same. I don't want you to let this worry consume you, baby girl. Let yourself mourn and don't put a timetable on it. Your hopes and fears are natural and I'd be feeling the same way if I were in your shoes."

She stepped back and placed her hands on his chest and he was sure she could feel the thump of his heart under her palms. "I don't think I could have done this without you."

Throwing caution to the wind, he pressed a kiss to her forehead and breathed in her heady scent. "You'll never have to know because I'll always be there if you need me."

Because he was a fool and an idiot who loved Arden way too much. He'd thought nothing could be worse than to be this close to her and not have her love, but he was wrong. The worst thing was not being near her at all.

"DO YOU WANT to get some lunch then?"

They'd knocked on Susannah's best friend's door but there was no answer, so now they were sitting in the rental car on the main drag of the little town after visiting the gravesite. Arden was paging through a few messages on her own phone and was feeling much better than she had at the cemetery. It was amazing how cathartic a good cry could be but she felt a hundred percent better.

She'd been too nervous to eat this morning and now found herself with a ravenous appetite. "Actually I'm starving, so that sounds good. Are we going to stay here and eat or go back into Indianapolis?"

Shane sighed and rubbed his chin, which only drew her attention to his square jaw covered in dark stubble. He'd always hated to shave and it looked like he'd skipped it this morning.

"That's an excellent question. Lydia Tate wasn't home and we don't really know where she is. Do you want to try again today or come back tomorrow?"

"I'd like to try again today but we can do anything you want."

Shane had already gone above and beyond the call of duty finding out the truth about her mother and father and then bringing her here. He'd been a tower of strength at the cemetery and she'd allowed herself to lean on him for a few minutes but all the while warning herself not to get too used to it.

"I'm at your command on this trip so we'll stay here in Hemingdale and kill some time before trying again. First, we eat and then we'll find something to do." He pointed to a restaurant on the corner of the block. "How about that little Italian place? Is that okay?"

It turned out to be perfect.

The hostess gave them a quiet table off to the side where they enjoyed a peaceful and delicious lunch. Shane had the spaghetti and meatballs while Arden ate every single bite of her baked ziti. She sat back and patted her stomach with a sigh.

"I shouldn't have eaten all that but it was so good."

Shane's own plate was clean and he was working on emptying the bread basket.

"It is good and there's no reason why you shouldn't have eaten it all. You didn't have any breakfast."

She'd love to be a size six again but that wasn't happening anytime in the near future. "I can't eat anything I want like I used to be able to. Women age and things change."

His hot gaze swept her from head to toe and she felt an answering warmth low in her abdomen. Damn, he was sexy as sin.

"You can't be worried about your figure. You look terrific."

His admiring regard had butterfly wings beating in her chest. It had been too long since anyone had looked at her like that and she'd missed it. She hadn't realized how much she needed it.

"Thank you, but I'm aware that is half a sentence. The other half is 'for a woman your age.' Men look at the twenty-somethings and pretty much ignore a female in her mid-thirties."

"You look good, period," he said bluntly. "You're a beautiful woman, Arden."

Funny how she didn't care if others thought she was beautiful but when this man said it…

"I'm older, so much older than you could possible know."

He frowned and she had to quell the urge to reach across the table and smooth the lines from his forehead. "I can count to fifteen."

He had no idea. She'd changed more than simply a few extra pounds and some lines around her eyes. When she'd left him that summer she'd been irrevocably changed.

"Men age so much better than women."

"That's one of the stupidest things I've ever heard and you ought to know better," he declared, not bothering to keep his voice down. "The only difference between men and women is that society allows men to age gracefully but society is full of shit. There's nothing more beautiful than a woman who has seen life and has learned to embrace it. Older women know what's important, and smooth skin and perky boobs aren't it, baby."

She stared at the table and traced patterns on the smooth

surface with her fingertip. "So the women you date are older?"

Her heart lurched at the thought of all the beautiful females he must have dated and made love to over the years. Had he been *in* love with any of them? Was there someone now that he cared about and wanted a future with?

"I haven't dated a woman under thirty in several years. I like being the immature one in the relationship."

Her lips quirked up at his joke. "Are you...dating someone? Is someone upset that you've come on this trip with me?"

Stupid. Stupid. Stop talking. He's going to figure out how I feel if I don't shut up.

"There's no need to worry about that. I'm a free agent and intend to stay that way."

"The original lone wolf?" she teased, relieved that there wasn't a woman waiting in the wings. "You always could charm the birds out of the trees, but then all the Anderson boys could too. Where's Leann these days?"

Leann was sister to Jason, West, and Travis and cousin to Shane. She was also the only female offspring in a bucketload of testosterone. She'd been in high school when Arden and Shane were dating.

Shane signaled for an ice tea refill for both of them. "She's living in Florida right now and from what I can tell she has no plans to come back any time soon. She sounds happy and that's the important thing, although her mom talks about wanting her married. Personally I think Leann saw the best and worst in her brothers and cousins and isn't in a big hurry to tie herself down."

"Like all the Andersons."

"I wouldn't say that. It just takes the right woman."

Biting her tongue, Arden managed to keep from asking if he'd ever found that woman and if he'd ever thought she might fit that description. He certainly had been "the one" for her and that hadn't changed no matter how hard she'd tried.

"I'm not sure I believe in soulmates," Arden said instead. "That's a tall order to ask one person to be everything. That seems like a lot of pressure."

Shane's smile fell and he suddenly seemed a million miles away from this booth in this restaurant. "If it's the right person then it's easy because they naturally are everything. They don't have to do anything special."

She didn't reply but turned her attention to her refilled glass. Taking a big gulp of ice tea, she choked slightly as an older woman leaned down over the table to stare at Arden.

Patting her chest, Arden coughed to clear her throat. "Um, can I help you?"

The well-dressed woman appeared to be in her late fifties or early sixties, with gray shot through her light brown hair and a few crinkles around her bright blue eyes.

"Arden?" the woman whispered as if she was afraid to speak up. "Is that you?"

Reaching across the table, Arden grabbed for Shane's hand, suddenly desperate for his calm strength. Her heart accelerated in her chest and it took all her effort to answer.

"Yes, I'm Arden. Do I know you?"

The woman's eyes filled with tears and her hand flew up to her mouth as a sob escaped her throat. "No, but I know you. You're the very picture of your mother."

Arden's gaze darted to Shane and then back to the woman.

"Did you know my mother?"

Maybe she would finally find out the truth and that scared the hell out of her.

The older woman blinked a few times and then smiled. "Honey, I'm your Auntie Lydia and your mother's best friend, and I can't tell you how much it means to me to see you after all of these years."

Chapter Twelve

LYDIA'S HAND GRIPPED Arden's tightly. "Child, you have no idea how many times a day I've thought about you and wondered how you were. You look so beautiful. Are you happy? Is this your husband?"

Her "aunt" had joined them at the table and Arden hadn't found the words to explain what they were doing in Hemingdale, but she had to try. Lydia might have the answers she wanted so desperately.

"Shane is my...friend." Arden felt the heat in her cheeks and didn't dare glance at him. "We were actually coming to see you but when we knocked on your door earlier you weren't there."

"Errands and things. I stopped in here to say hello to the owner who is a good friend of mine." Lydia smiled widely and shook her head. "My goodness, can you imagine if I hadn't? I would have missed you!"

"We were planning to come back by tonight," Shane replied smoothly. "There's no way we would have left without seeing you, Mrs. Tate."

"Please call me Lydia and I'll call you Shane. Is that all right?"

"Absolutely. Lydia," Shane began, casting an inquiring glance in Arden's direction before continuing. She was happy to let him take the lead here as words seemed to be stuck in her throat. "We're here because Arden's father has disappeared and when we went to investigate we found that he'd changed his and Arden's last name and moved to Tremont. We also found out about how her mother died and you can imagine what a shock it was."

Eyes wide, Lydia sucked in a breath. "You didn't know? But Ben said he'd tell you when you grew up." The older woman snorted and her lips pressed tightly together. "But then he also said he'd send us pictures and updates of your life and that didn't happen. He cut us out like a surgeon and told us that it was for the best and that we'd just upset you."

That sounded like Benjamin Cavendish, always having to be in control of every detail and every person right down to their emotions. When she saw him again they were going to have a long talk.

"We were hoping you could tell Arden about her mother and her life here. According to the investigation, Arden also has an uncle?"

The color drained from Lydia's face and she clutched the edge of the table. "Yes, that's true but there's time to talk about that later. Why don't you come over to the house and we can relax and talk? I have so many things to tell you and I want to hear all about your life, child."

Thrilled and scared at the same time, Arden nodded in agreement. She wanted to know and that's why she was here. What was that saying?

The truth will set you free.

✦   ✦   ✦

SHANE STOOD BY the back window of Lydia's living room watching as the two women pored over photo albums. Arden had shed a few tears but seemed to be holding herself together well as Lydia pointed out pictures from their childhood and told stories of backyard barbecues, summers at the lake, and building snowmen at Christmastime.

His heart ached that she'd missed out on all this with her own mother but she'd never once complained the entire time he'd known her. She'd taken her motherless status as a simple fact of life and thrown all her love and admiration toward her father.

Sometimes too much.

Lydia pointed to a large eight-by-ten photo. "This was Susie on her prom night. Her daddy was quite scandalized that her neckline was cut so low but Susie wouldn't have any other dress. The minute she saw it in the store she knew it was the one."

Arden giggled as her fingers traced the lines of the picture. "Father looks so young in this photo."

Lydia raised her stricken gaze to Shane and her lips trembled as if she wanted to speak but didn't quite know what to say. Her face had paled again just as when they were in the restaurant and his intuition was going off like a car alarm. There was much more to this story than what he'd seen in the file from Jason.

Easing himself onto the sofa next to Arden, he pressed his hand over hers in a comforting gesture but knew it wasn't going to be nearly enough. Whatever had Lydia so upset was bad. Very bad.

Licking her dry lips, Lydia took a shaky breath before speaking. "That's not Ben—that's David, his brother."

He hadn't seen that coming at all.

Frowning, Arden leaned closer to study the photo. "David? That's my uncle?"

"Your mother and David dated for a few years."

His eyes met Lydia's and he saw the anguish in their depths. Clearly this part of Susannah's story was painful for all involved.

"But she married my dad." Shane could practically see the wheels turning in Arden's head. "How did that happen?"

Lydia sighed and patted Arden's knee. "I'm not sure where to start. It's hard to explain but I'll try. I guess I'll start at the beginning."

"Where is the beginning?" Arden asked, moving closer to Shane and he wrapped his arm around her shoulders.

"David was the older brother," Lydia began. "He was good-looking and wild. Exciting, I guess is how he would have been described. He liked to drink, take drugs, drive fast, and party until the wee hours of the morning. Susie loved him but after high school he would disappear for days at a time and his explanations when he came back left something to be desired. She was afraid that David was cheating on her and they started to argue quite a bit. Eventually they broke up and Ben was waiting in the wings. He'd had a crush on Susie for years and he took that opportunity to sweep her off her feet. Within six months they were engaged and a year later they were married. It was a good thing too, as David's behavior became increasingly more erratic and there were rumors that he had a secret girlfriend and baby in Indianapolis."

Arden leaned into him, her head on his shoulder. Her breath was shallow and her skin appeared pasty and gray. "That's why he never spoke about his own brother. He stole David's girl-friend."

Lydia stood and walked over to the fireplace, running her fingers over the framed photos on the mantle. "That isn't why he didn't mention David." She sighed heavily and briefly buried her head in her hands. "God, I never thought I would have to tell you this. I thought Ben would have told you."

Shane didn't imagine the bitterness in Lydia's tone. Appar-ently Ben could piss people off here in Hemingdale as well as in Tremont.

"Please understand that your mother's life wasn't always easy. Her marriage to Ben wasn't working and the strain was showing. They fought all the time and usually when David was back in town. She still loved him." The older woman whispered the last four words.

Stiffening in his arms, Arden sucked in a breath. "She was in love with David?"

Lydia nodded, tears shining in her blue eyes. "She tried to be a good wife to Ben but he wasn't an easy man to love. While David was wild he was also charming. Ben was moody and difficult, plus had a nasty temper. When he traveled on business, Susie would visit with David. At first I think it truly was inno-cent but later…"

The implication was clear. Susannah and David were having an affair. Had Ben known?

"How did my mother die?" Arden asked softly, obviously

still in shock from her aunt's revelation.

Her hands wrung together, Lydia allowed a few tears to streak down her cheeks. "Ben was out of town on a business trip and Susie was home alone with just you. According to the police, somewhere between eleven and midnight someone entered through the unlocked back door and shot her twice in the chest as she exited the bathroom. Neighbors heard the shots and you crying and called 911."

Arden drew a shuddering breath, her trembling hands reaching for Shane's. He pulled her more tightly against him, feeling her entire body shake in reaction to the story.

"Who did it?"

Wiping away the tears, her aunt shook her head sadly. "They never caught the animal. A few people said they saw David running away from the scene but after they questioned him they didn't have any evidence. There were others that swore he was across town drinking in a bar and playing pool when the murder happened. Eventually David left town under a cloud of suspicion, never to be heard from again."

"And Daddy changed our names and moved away," finished Arden in a choked voice. "I wouldn't even know any of this if he hadn't disappeared last week. I'd be completely clueless."

"However misguided it may seem now, at the time, we all agreed it was the best thing for you. We didn't want you to grow up in this little town being the daughter of the woman who was murdered and the killer was never found. It would have followed you your entire life and we wanted to spare you that. What we didn't realize was that Ben was going to cut us out of your life completely and that we would become strangers to you here in

Hemingdale. That was never part of the plan, Arden—please believe me. Even though you weren't here I never stopped loving you or being your honorary aunt. You've had a Christmas gift under the tree every year in this house. I still have them all."

Pale and trembling in his arms, Arden laid her head on his shoulder. "I think...I could use a drink."

"I think we all could," replied Shane. "I don't suppose you have some brandy or whiskey, Lydia?"

The older woman smiled and stood. "Actually I do have a nice brandy and you're right, I think we all could use a snort. It must be five o'clock somewhere."

Lydia disappeared into another room and Shane tipped Arden's chin up so she was looking into his eyes. "Are you okay, princess? What do you need from me?"

"Don't let me go."

Her stark admission cut straight to his heart. He'd be there for her in any way she needed him, at any time. She might not be his to love but she was his to care for and protect. At least while they were here.

Chapter Thirteen

"I WANT TO hire your cousin Jason and his partners."

Arden had waited until she and Shane had returned to the hotel after spending the afternoon and evening catching up on the last thirty years with Aunt Lydia. Immediately, she'd felt close to the older woman and vowed to stay in touch no matter what. In fact, Lydia wanted to throw a party in Arden's honor so she could meet the residents of the small town she would have grown up in.

Retrieving a beer from the minibar, Shane sat down on the couch before answering.

"They're not a private investigations firm. Their true function is to consult with law enforcement on difficult cases."

"This one qualifies, don't you think? Unsolved for decades and barely a suspect in sight. I know what they – and you – are capable of and I need their help. I want to find my mother's killer."

Shane gave her a patient look. "I'm still in the middle of the other thing you asked me to do. We still haven't found your father."

She walked over to him, lifted the bottle from his grip, and took a long drag from it. He looked shocked for a moment, then threw back his head and laughed before heading back to the minibar for another beer.

"That's the girl I knew. Every now and then I see glimpses of her. She knew how to kick ass and take names."

"That girl is a woman and she's damn tired of people keeping important secrets like this from her. I need the truth and I need to find my mother's killer so she can rest in peace."

A long-suffering sigh escaped from Shane's lips. "If I don't help, you'll just try and do it yourself, won't you?"

She wouldn't have a clue as to where to even start but she'd try. "It would be easier if Jason's firm helped me."

His lips curved into a smile. "Then it's a good thing I already sent him a text and asked him to start looking for David Hollis, isn't it? I also thought tomorrow we could go to the police station and look at the case file, maybe even re-interview any witnesses if they're still in Hemingdale."

She couldn't help herself. She launched herself at him, their bodies colliding with a thud and a giggle. He wrapped his arms around her middle and lifted her off the ground. "How did you know I was going to ask? Have you become a mind reader since I last saw you?"

Chuckling, he set her on her feet and reached for his beer, leaving her feeling slightly at a loss. It had felt so amazingly wonderful to be that close to him and not be in tears as if the world was ending. "Hardly. But I watched your expression as your aunt told the story. I knew you wouldn't be satisfied if you didn't try and solve the mystery and I'd be a total jerk if I didn't help you."

Her smile fell and she stepped back. She'd asked so much from him and given so little in return. "You've done more than I could ever have hoped for, Shane. More than I deserve. I know that you hate me and well…honestly I don't blame you."

Pain flickered across his features but was almost instantly gone. If she hadn't seen it with her own two eyes she wouldn't have believed it.

"I don't hate you, baby girl. But if you want to pay me back you can. You can tell me – once and for all – why you left that summer. All I want is the truth. Can you do that for me?"

She owed it to him. She needed to do it.

But damn, it would change everything. He wouldn't look at her the same anymore and she wasn't sure she could stand that but this wasn't about her.

"I will tell you," she finally said, the words catching in her throat. "But not tonight, okay?"

"That's fine. Take the time that you need. You know where I am."

She had a reprieve but it wouldn't last for long. The truth of that summer couldn't be swept under the rug any longer. She'd tell him everything.

✦　✦　✦

SHANE HAD BEEN surprised by how easy it had been to convince the police to show them the file, especially as it was still considered an open investigation. He couldn't help but wonder if perhaps one of Jason's partners had contacts that had smoothed their path.

Either way, they were now sitting in a tiny gray conference

room in the police station perusing the contents. He leafed through the Susannah Hollis murder police file with a heavy heart and growing frustration. It was easily the skimpiest evidence he'd ever seen and it was no wonder that they'd never found the shooter.

"There's not much here. They didn't find any fingerprints that didn't belong. They were able to recover the bullet but it didn't match anything in the system. All the witnesses had conflicting statements as well. Not a whole lot to go on here."

Arden set down one of the witness statements and sighed. "This is disheartening. It's like they immediately gave up. As far as I can see they only spoke to a few people."

"They did speak to your uncle but didn't question him about his relationship with your mother. He simply gave a statement that he was out drinking and playing pool, which a few other people corroborated. But then how do you explain a neighbor saying she saw him get in his car and drive away from the house after the shots were fired?"

"People see what they want to see," she reminded him. "If they were having an affair they might have met at the house when my father was out of town. As my uncle, he wouldn't raise any suspicions."

Arden had been remarkably calm this morning and Shane wasn't sure he could trust it. If she needed to scream, yell, or cry, he didn't mind but this serene mask was kind of disturbing. It was like waiting for the other shoe to drop.

"Are you okay about all this?" he questioned. "I'm worried about you."

Her fingers fiddled with the empty paper cup from the coffee joint around the corner and her eyes wouldn't meet his gaze.

"I'm still processing everything. I'm trying to stay sort of separate from it all as if this is happening to someone else. It's like I'm looking down on my body in a way. I am upset but I know that crying and bemoaning my lot in life isn't going to help anything. It's best if I try and stick to business."

It sounded like she was going to have one hell of a breakdown at some point. He only hoped he would be there to help her through it and come out stronger on the other side.

"You're doing a great job staying calm but just remember you don't need to. No one would blame you if you took up smoking or drinking right about now."

She tossed the empty cup into a small trashcan. "I've always wanted to take up skydiving. Maybe this is my lucky day."

She forgot he knew her too well. "Bullshit. You're terrified of heights. I never could get you to climb rocks with us. You don't even like to be on a ladder."

"It is smart to be afraid of heights," she huffed. "A person could get seriously injured or die if they fall. It's survival of the fittest. You, sir, are going against nature."

There was that smile and giggle again. Dammit, he loved it when she dropped the serious facade and played. Just a little.

"Maybe I'm simply more evolved and I'm not afraid anymore. Have you thought about that?"

Tapping the file folder, she rolled her eyes and groaned. "Can we get back to the case now?"

Shane shrugged and grinned. "Sure, if you don't have a good answer we can. I think we should talk to some of these witnesses again if we can find them. See if they stick to their story."

"I had an answer but I'm not going to let you bait me."

Shane jotted down the names and addresses in a notebook. "Seems like you already have."

"You haven't changed a bit. I've got teenagers in my classes that are more mature than you are."

He closed the file folder and tucked the notebook in his jacket pocket. "That wouldn't surprise me, but then my joie de vivre is one of the reasons people love me. I'm fun."

Crossing her arms over her chest, she lifted an eyebrow in question. "Fun?"

"That's right. And might I say that you seem to be in desperate need of some. When was the last time you had fun, Arden? I mean real belly-laughing, gut-busting, I almost peed my pants fun."

The bravado she'd been displaying seeped out of her like air out of a balloon, and she sat there shoulders slumped in defeat. "I don't remember."

He couldn't stand on the sidelines and let that sad state continue.

"Task number one. Have fun. Task number two. Talk to witnesses. So put on your coat and we can get going. We have a full day ahead of us."

He didn't know what they were going to do yet but it was going to be something to remember. At least for him. One more chance to have a wonderful day with the woman he loved.

Chapter Fourteen

ARDEN WAS HAVING the time of her life.

When Shane had explained where he was taking them she'd been dubious but the reality certainly surpassed any of her expectations. He'd found what was known as an "escape room" where people paid for the privilege of being locked into a themed room and had to find a way out with puzzles and clues. Their room had been Sherlock Holmes's study and it had been quite a challenge.

She and Shane had been grouped with a few other people and the "host" explained that there were four different puzzles, each color-coded – yellow, blue, green, and red. Participants had to find all the clues in the room for each puzzle and they were marked with a colored sticker. Then they would use the clues to solve the puzzles and unlock the door. All in sixty minutes.

Except it didn't quite work that way.

First, because they didn't know the people they'd been grouped with, working together was a bit difficult. They tried but the fact was the others didn't seem all that thrilled to even be there, let alone rip apart every nook and cranny of a room for clues.

Second, and this part was rather humiliating, Arden found out she sucked at puzzles. Shane's ability was top-notch but her own was severely lacking. She had always considered herself an intelligent person but when standing in front of those puzzles with those vague clues she'd been stumped. If it hadn't been for Shane, it would have gone quite badly. Luckily they managed to solve two of the puzzles completely and almost finished the other two.

Which meant the host had to let them out of the room and tell them what they missed.

"I want to go again," Arden pouted as they scarfed down a couple of burgers shortly afterward. "I'll do better next time."

"Now that you know where all the clues are and what they mean?" Shane smirked. "I think we'd both do better. You didn't do all that bad. I've been to one before but in a different city, so I had an idea as to what to expect. You did well for your first time."

Arden giggled as she remembered bumbling through the puzzles. "I did a terrible job but it was still fun. When did you do it before?"

Streaks of red painted Shane's cheeks and his gaze dropped to his burger. "During a trip to Los Angeles."

Her own heart dropped to her feet before she mentally gave herself a slap. If he'd gone on a date with a woman it wasn't any of her business. She ought to be happy for him. She was the one that left, after all. She should be thrilled he hadn't spent the ensuing years pining for her.

Craptastic.

Except that she didn't like thinking of him with another female. Holding her, kissing her. Maybe even telling her he loved her. The last one hurt the most of all.

It was best to divert the conversation before they treaded on shaky – and personal – ground.

"This was a wonderful break. Thank you for taking me. I do feel better."

Shane looked up and grinned, showing off that Anderson dimple in his cheek and looking more handsome than anyone had a right to.

"We're not even close to being done today. There's more magical fun to come."

She should have known. Shane always took things to extremes. He wouldn't be happy with an hour of games and then a cheeseburger.

"What do you have up your sleeve?" Arden shook a fry at him playfully. "I'm actually kind of scared right now."

Waggling his eyebrows, he picked up one if his fries and pretended it was a sword, dueling with her own until he popped it in his mouth. "You can never have too much fun, so prepare yourself, darlin'."

Arden was scared but not of having a good time. She was afraid of falling even further in love with the grown-up Shane Anderson. That would be a tragedy she could never come back from.

✦ ✦ ✦

"IT'S COLD OUT here," Arden hissed, zipping her jacket all the way to her chin. "I think you've officially lost your mind, Shane Anderson."

It was a distinct possibility but he'd had too much fun today to care. After they had spent a delightful afternoon trying to escape from Sherlock Holmes's study, he dragged her to a burger joint where they'd filled up on hamburgers and fries. They'd barely digested their dinner when he'd driven them to a miniature golf course with a shipwreck theme.

And Arden was beating the pants off of him. And smiling.

The sun had set and the temperature had dropped quite a bit, especially for this early in the season but they were still enjoying themselves.

"Stop whining and just putt, woman," Shane chuckled. "I think this hole is where I'm going to make my comeback, so be prepared."

Swinging her club playfully, she lined up the shot with the red golf ball. Shane's was blue and he could have sworn he heard her mutter something under her breath about that.

To make the shot, she had to swing the ball through a narrow passage on the left so it would glide down a steep hill, bank off of the far edge and then hopefully land right in the hole. So far, she'd managed less than three strokes on each of the eight holes they'd played so far, including two holes in one. She was some sort of mini-golf savant.

"Watch and learn, Anderson. Watch and learn."

She was awesome but that didn't mean he had to make it easy for her. He was an Anderson boy and that meant he was competitive as hell.

"You aren't nervous, are you?" he asked as she addressed the ball. "You're not feeling the pressure, are you? Because it's just a game. It's not like the PGA championship is on the line or actual cash money."

She had been staring at the ball but now she lifted her head slightly to look at him. "God, you're annoying. I'm not nervous or feeling the pressure. Why would I?"

She bent her head again but then quickly looked up. "What do you mean about money? We're not betting here."

Shane leaned casually on his putter and shrugged. "Of course not. Unless…you want to. Make a bet, I mean."

Straightening, she pushed a stray curl behind her ear. "A bet? For money? How much?"

He had her distracted; now he needed to go in for the kill.

"Money…or something else."

Her gaze narrowed and she shook the putter in his direction, causing him to have to hide his laughter. She was cute when she was intense.

"What did you have in mind, Anderson? I'll kick your butt from here to Tremont, so make it something good."

He hadn't actually had anything in mind. He just liked messing with her and getting her all feisty.

"If I win, you provide maid and chef service every day for a week. If you win, you can choose whatever prize you want."

She wouldn't choose what he'd like to give her – himself and a whole lot of pleasure – but if she had him as her maid then he'd get to spend more time with her while spoiling her a little.

She'd needed fun today but she could use some tender loving care as well. Not to mention a break from all the melodrama in her life.

"A maid and chef," Arden smirked. "You are so going down. I can't wait to see your big macho self do the laundry and scrub the floors. You're on."

Getting back into position, she pulled back the putter and gave the ball a controlled smack. It veered instantly to the left, sliding through the passage and down the hill before hitting the wooden side of the putting green and rolling toward the hole. He heard Arden's swift intake of breath as it moved ever closer…closer…and then…stopped.

Two inches from the hole.

"Horse poop," she muttered under her breath, her shoulders slumping slightly before whirling around and showing off a dazzling smile. "Beat that, Anderson. If you can."

"You are an evil woman, baby girl. You're enjoying watching me squirm, aren't you? That's not the action of a sweet little school teacher."

She pursed her lips as if angry but her cheeks were rosy with mirth. "I'm going to squash you like a bug. My grout needs cleaning, slave boy."

Whistling a lilting tune, he gently elbowed her out of the way. "My turn to dazzle and amaze. You might want to talk to someone, sweetheart. You have a real aggression problem that you should be worried about."

She coughed a few times. "Dazzle." Cough. "Amaze." Cough. Cough.

Shane lined up the shot and gave the ball a firm hit, but it must have been with the tip of the club and not the middle because it careened to the right, hitting embedded rocks before coming to a sad halt at least twenty feet from the hole.

How do you clean grout anyway?

He gave Arden a hard look and wagged his finger. "Not a

word, do you hear me? Not a damn word."

Pressing her lips together to keep from laughing in his face, she waltzed past him, her hips swaying and pulling his attention from his imminent defeat. They had nine more holes to go but if he was able to walk right behind her while she wore those snug blue jeans, it would all be worth it.

"Do you want me to go again so my ball is out of the way?" she asked.

Shane eyed the shot he needed to make and it wasn't pretty. He was getting his ass royally kicked but it was totally worth it.

"Fine, but you're buying ice cream when we're done here. Hot fudge and whipped cream too."

He wanted to make this day last as long as possible.

TUCKED INTO BED again, Arden strained to hear any movement from Shane upstairs. She'd heard the thump of his boots when he'd kicked them off, and the sound of running water when he'd taken a quick shower and brushed his teeth. But now that they were both in bed, the silence in the room seemed to stretch on forever.

Today had reminded her of all the reasons she'd fallen in love with Shane to begin with. Charming and fun, he radiated complete acceptance of whomever he was with. It had been such a change from her day to day life with her father. Ben had pushed her to achieve in school and in extra-curricular clubs to the point she'd almost mutinied several times. Her teen years had been filled with angst at never being good enough for her father. It had been a breath of fresh air to meet Shane and be told she was enough just as she was.

She'd also seen the keen intelligence today that had surprised her when they first started dating. He'd been known as something of a playboy, so she hadn't expected a guy who could spout Shakespeare and help her with her physics homework. Combined with a soft heart and buckets of kindness, he'd seemed like the world's most perfect boyfriend.

Here we go again.

Somehow, these last fifteen years she'd managed not to think about him every single day, although it hadn't been easy. So many things reminded her of him and each time it felt like a dagger to the heart when a memory or image had taken up residence in her brain.

They say time heals all wounds but hers had never quite gone away. She'd compared every man to Shane.

They'd all came up wanting in some way, even her husband. Both she and Michael had known they weren't a great love affair when they'd married but she'd thought they could make something of their life with respect and friendship. How wrong she'd been. Respect and friendship had quickly turned to something else as he'd turned to woman after woman to slake his need for constant attention. One woman simply hadn't been enough for him. He'd craved the admiration of a thousand female gazes and Arden didn't want to be one in a crowd when it came to her own husband.

She'd known she'd never stopped loving Shane. Not really. But what she hadn't expected when he agreed to help her was that she would start falling for him – as an adult – all over again.

Like every other female in Tremont. And that was something she simply couldn't allow herself to be.

Chapter Fifteen

T HE NEXT MORNING Shane drove down the residential street
and checked the address again before pulling over. He
pointed to the large, two-story Tudor with a circular driveway
and large shade trees on the front lawn.

"That's where your mother and father lived."

Arden didn't know how she was supposed to feel. She didn't
have any memories of that time in her life so there was no
emotion as she stared at the home. There was only the strange
feeling anyone would get when staring at the location of a
gruesome crime.

"Do you think the new owners will let us in?"

Shane shrugged and exited the rental car before coming
around to her side to open the door. "I'm not sure, but I'd like
to get a look at the scene since there weren't any photos in the
police file."

They walked up the path and Shane rang the doorbell as Arden looked around, not sure what she thought she might see. It
had been over thirty years and any clue would be long gone.
Maybe she simply wanted something to remember her mother
by but this was probably not the place for that if she wanted it to

be a pleasant memory.

"They're on vacation."

A woman's voice came out of nowhere and Arden did a three-sixty trying to find where it came from. A tiny older female popped out from behind a rose bush wearing gardening gloves and a kind smile. Shane stepped forward and held out his hand.

"Hello, I'm Shane Anderson and this is Arden Hollis. You must be Delilah Ward, the next door neighbor."

Delilah Ward had been on the list of witnesses in the police file, which was good. But Arden wasn't sure it was good that he'd referred to herself as 'Hollis' since that wasn't her name any longer, but there wasn't much sense in keeping her identity a secret. When Aunt Lydia had her party everyone would know.

The old woman's face lit up and she clapped her hands together. "Arden! Look at you, all grown up. You've become such a beautiful woman and so like your mother." The smile fell immediately. "Such a sad thing. I have to ask what you're doing back here. This can't be a happy place for you, dear."

"We're hoping you can help us, actually." Shane gave Delilah his most charming smile. That one that had females' panties dissolving in seconds and it appeared to work on women of all ages, if Delilah's blush was anything to go by. "Arden and I are trying to find out a little more about her mother's untimely passing. Were you home that night? Do you remember anything?"

Delilah slowly took off her gloves and sighed. "I think that conversation needs to be had sitting down. How about a glass of ice tea? I made some oatmeal cookies this morning and they're still warm."

"That's my favorite cookie," Arden offered. "We appreciate your time, Mrs. Ward."

"Call me Del. Everyone does." She waved them forward. "Let's go in the house then. Just ignore Sammy. He doesn't know he's a cat, thinks he's a puppy."

It was love at first sight when Sammy laid eyes on Shane. As soon as they were seated, the feline jumped into Shane's lap and curled up for a nap. Luckily, he didn't seem to mind and scratched the tabby cat behind the ear while Del went into the kitchen.

Arden tried to relax but it was difficult when she was unsure as to what Del was going to say. She'd had so many shocking revelations in the past week she wasn't sure her heart could take one more, but she had a nasty suspicion that was she'd learned was only the beginning.

"Can I help you, Del?" Arden stood and reached for the tray, setting it on the coffee table in front of the sofa where she and Shane sat.

"Thank you, dear. You're very kind." Del perched on the edge of a chair to Shane's right and held out a plate of cookies. "Please help yourself."

They both took one and a glass of tea but refreshments weren't uppermost in Arden's mind. She wanted – no, needed – to know if Del had any memories of that night.

"These are good." Shane had taken a big bite and groaned with pleasure. "I'm going to have to have a second one."

Del smiled with happiness. "There's plenty. I just love a man with a hearty appetite. My George could put away a big dinner and a slab of chocolate cake in the blink of an eye. Nowadays, he doesn't eat so much. We just have the one big meal midday and snacks for dinner."

Arden looked around but didn't see anyone else. "Is he here?"

"Down at the center playing chess with some of his friends. He'll be home soon. Now you wanted to know about the night your mother died? Such a sad affair. And they never found who did it either. So tragic."

Shane stroked the cat and its furry tail curled around his hand. "Can you remember anything about that night, Del? Anything at all?"

Del laughed and set down her glass. "The funny thing about getting older is I sometimes don't remember why I went into the kitchen but I can remember Christmas when I was eight years old. So yes, I do remember that night. George and I were sitting here after dinner watching 'Dallas' on television. That J.R. Ewing was such a rascal. Anyway, when we were sitting here we heard what sounded to me like the backfiring of a car. But George said right away that he thought it was gunshots and he would know as he was in the Korean War. I couldn't believe there could be anyone shooting in our neighborhood so I walked out onto the porch, which of course got me yelled at by my husband."

"George was correct. If there was an active shooter situation then being outside wasn't a good idea," Shane said. "Best to stay indoors and call 911."

"Back then we'd never heard of an active shooter situation, son."

Good point. Things had changed in the last thirty-plus years.

"That's true. Go on."

"I stood on my front porch for quite a while, waiting to see if I would hear any more but there was only silence. Then maybe five or ten minutes later I saw a man run from the house and get in a car parked a few blocks down."

Arden's grip had tightened on the couch cushion, her knuckles white with tension. Hearing the story firsthand was turning out to be more intense than reading about it in a police report.

"Did you recognize that man?" Shane asked, placing a reassuring hand on Arden's thigh and giving it a light squeeze. She placed her own hand over his and entwined their fingers together. If anyone had told her a few weeks ago she would be spending this much time with Shane voluntarily and even allowing herself to touch and hug him she would have said they were crazy. But in a few short days, he'd managed to sneak under all her defenses.

"It was dark but most of the porch lights were on all down the street, so I got a good look. It was David Hollis. I'd seen him come and go ever since Ben and Susannah moved in. He and Ben had a difficult relationship but he doted on you, Arden. He never came over empty-handed. He always had a doll or a stuffed animal. He liked to sit with you out in the backyard while you played."

Frustrated she couldn't remember any of this, Arden fidgeted in her seat. Jason's firm was looking for her uncle but this story made her want to meet him more than ever. Anger at her father bubbled in her abdomen as she thought about all he'd robbed her of. Family. Heritage. Perhaps when she'd been a child she could see the reason but she'd been an adult for a long time now.

Shane leaned over, his elbows on his knees. "You spent a lot of time with Susannah and Ben?"

Del scrunched up her face for a moment. "Not Ben. He was traveling so much for work. But Susannah? Yes, I did. She was a new mother and needed the support of someone who had some experience. We'd have coffee several times a week and I babysat many times. If the weather was good we'd sit out on the front porch just visiting. She was a sweet woman but I could tell she wasn't happy with Ben. You could hear them fighting when the windows were open. I told the police that but they said Ben was out of town."

Shane pounced on Del's statement. "You think Ben had a reason to kill Susannah?"

Not even realizing she'd been holding her breath, Arden painfully exhaled when Del nodded. Her hand fluttered to cover her mouth as if she was about to say a dirty word.

"He had a few reasons. One was money of course. From my understanding, she had a large trust fund from her father Charles although I never discussed it with her nor did she act like she had a lot of money. With Ben struggling with his business that must have been tempting to say the least."

Arden's father had never mentioned a trust fund the few times he'd spoken about his wife but then he'd lied so often she couldn't believe anything anymore.

"What was the other reason?" Shane asked, glancing quickly at Arden.

"Everyone knew…you know…about her and David."

"Everyone?" Arden heard herself echoing. "Even my father?"

"I don't see how he couldn't have known, dear. It was the

talk of Hemingdale society. But I can't say for sure, of course. Susannah and I never spoke of the situation."

"But Daddy was out of town?"

Del nodded. "Yes, that's what the police said."

"What about David?" Shane queried. "If he ran from the house shortly after Susannah was shot, you'd think he'd be suspect number one."

"The newspapers said he wasn't actually here," Del replied with a snort. "That he was over at the Lone Wolf Lounge tying one on and playing pool. There were witnesses and even a…ahem…lady of the evening who said he spent the night with her. But I know what I saw. It was David Hollis. I'm sure of it."

A love affair gone wrong? Had David Hollis taken Arden's mother's life?

Or had Ben murdered his own wife to get his hands on her trust fund?

She had to find her uncle and father to get any answers.

Chapter Sixteen

AUNT LYDIA'S COCKTAIL party that evening was in full swing, and from what Shane could see it looked like the entire town of Hemingdale had scored an invite. The house was bursting to the seams with bodies and he'd been introduced to so many that there was no way he would remember their names ten minutes later. Luckily most of the guests weren't all that interested in him.

They wanted to meet Arden.

She was the star of the party and from the way people were eyeing her up and down, Shane could see why Ben had taken her away and given her a new life. No one had yet been so gauche as to bring up the murder, but he could see it in the way they looked at her, that wondering.

How much did she know? Did her father do it? Or her uncle?

Shane's job tonight was to be a shield between her and everyone else. If anyone stepped one toe out of line he'd be stomping on it with a sledgehammer. Arden was happy and smiling, and nothing and no one was going to ruin that for her.

He grasped her hand and pulled her off to the side of the

room. "Can I get you another drink? Something to eat?"

She held out her empty martini glass. "I am thirsty but no more alcohol. I don't want to get drunk or even tipsy in front of a bunch of people I just met. Maybe a soda?"

Shane's gaze swept the room before returning to Arden. "I think they'd love it. It would give them something to gossip about. As it is, I think we're something of a disappointment. You're too normal and not here with a raving lunatic."

"They don't know you like I do."

He bopped her on the top of her nose with a finger. She'd managed to put her melancholy aside for the party and was in a good mood. "You're becoming awfully saucy these last few days. You have quite the mouth on you at times."

One shoulder lifted carelessly in her black cocktail dress that they'd spent the afternoon shopping for in Indianapolis. "You love it and you know it."

Chuckling, Shane gave her a triumphant smile. "I do. Now that drink…"

He left her chatting with Lydia's daughter Megan while he procured two fresh drinks and a plate of finger foods. By the time he returned, Arden's sunny expression had turned to storm clouds. Clearly, Shane had been gone too long and needed to intervene.

Now.

Setting the two glasses and plate down on an end table to his right, he slid his arm around Arden's shoulders. "What happened? You look ready to kick someone in the balls."

Her lips were tight and her blue eyes gray with anger. "Men are pigs."

"Pretty much." Arguing that point would get him nowhere when she was in this mood. "Did one in particular say or do something that I need to punch them in the gut for? Just point him out."

Groaning and rolling her eyes, Arden picked up her drink and took a sip. "I can fight my own battles. It's just there is always at least one in every crowd. That guy that thinks that every woman wants him and is just waiting for a sign."

"Some guy gave you the sign, huh? What did you do?"

"He said that maybe I might want to go somewhere with him after the party. To…you know…get to know one another better. He leaned close to me and ran his hand down my arm. Ick. I told him that I was planning to wash my hair and read a magazine."

"Ouch. Did he back down?"

"He saw you coming this way and darted outside, probably to lick his wounds. Why are men such jerks? I don't even know him. Why would he think I'd want to go anywhere with him?"

Shane could spend the rest of the night and the next day lecturing her about the delicate psyche of the hunter-male but he doubted Arden would be interested.

"It's a numbers game, sweetheart," he said instead. "If he comes on to a bunch of women then one might be interested. He doesn't care about getting shot down."

"He was creepy," Arden declared with a shudder. "He needs to learn to keep his hands to himself."

Yes, he did and Shane was just the man to teach him that lesson. He motioned across the room to Lydia who was having an animated conversation with the local banker. Or maybe he was a lawyer. Shane couldn't remember. It was one of the two.

Lydia joined them and gave Arden a big hug. "You two look like you're having fun. I'm so glad I gave this party. Everyone is so thrilled to meet you."

Arden hugged her aunt back, the smile returning to her face. "And thank you for having us. This evening has been such fun and so interesting. I've met so many new people."

"I completely agree. If you don't mind," Shane cut in smoothly. "I'd like to circle back around with someone from earlier. Would you ladies excuse me for just a moment?"

Both women nodded and launched into a discussion about how no one gave cocktail parties anymore. Shane ducked out of the house onto the back porch and saw his quarry. A lone man puffing on a cigarette leaned against the deck railing, blowing puffs of smoke into the chilly night air.

Shane sidled up about three feet away, still sipping at his whiskey. "Great party, huh?"

"Lydia always gives great parties. Best booze and food around."

The words were slightly slurred. Arden's not-so-prince-charming was well on his way to being drunk.

"I can see that. Plus some beautiful women too."

The man's face broke into a smile and he leaned more heavily on the railing as he tossed his cigarette away. "You've got that right but some of them are real bitches. You know what I mean?"

Shane moved in closer so he was invading the drunk's physical space. The sandy-haired man was shorter than Shane by about six inches and had to crane his neck to see Shane's face.

"You mean like when you touch a woman that doesn't want

you and doesn't belong to you?" Shane stepped closer, their chests bumping. "Is that what you mean?"

The man's mouth fell open, gaping like a fish but no words came out.

"Because if a woman doesn't want you that doesn't make her a bitch or whatever colorful name you've come up with to make yourself feel better. It might be a good idea if you didn't go around propositioning women who don't show any interest in you to begin with."

The drunk was unsteady on his feet as he tried to put distance between them. "Man, she came on to me, not the other way around. If I'd known she was yours, I'd have stayed away."

At least the guy hadn't been doing this to other women all night. He'd singled out Arden for his attentions.

"She's a human being, not a dog, so she doesn't belong to anyone but herself." Shane got right in his face, nose to nose, to make his point. "And she didn't come on to you, asshole, and we both know it, so don't even try that one with me. I really think you should pour yourself into a cab and go home and sober up before you do something else that's even more stupid. Like punching me. I know you're thinking about it. That would be a huge mistake, my friend."

The drunk's red face spoke volumes and for a moment Shane thought the man was going to take a swing. Eventually he must have thought better of it and he backed down, muttering a few not so nice words, before staggering into the house.

Shane chuckled to himself and sucked in a lungful of fresh air, the temperature much more mild than the previous night. He should probably go back in but the evening was pleasant and

Arden was in Lydia's more than competent hands. The older woman was as protective as Shane was.

"Did you scare that man?"

Turning on his heel, Shane grinned as he watched a smirking Arden approach. "I did and I don't regret it. I wasn't going to hit him or anything. All we did was chat for a few minutes."

She joined him at the railing, her light floral perfume mixing with the aroma of freshly cut grass. He didn't stop himself from reaching out and tucking a stray curl behind her ear and letting his fingertips linger a moment too long on her satin cheek.

Fuck being a gentleman.

Fuck getting his heart broken.

Fuck keeping his distance.

She was gorgeous tonight and he could barely peel his gaze away from her. Her beauty practically glowed and everyone could see it tonight. Part of him wanted to hide her away just for himself, and the other part wanted to show her off. It was primitive, almost caveman-like behavior and it didn't make any damn sense. After all, she wasn't his to hide or display.

"And then he ran into the house like the devil himself was on his heels. What exactly did you say to him, Shane?"

"I just said that perhaps he should keep his hands to himself when the lady wasn't interested."

He felt her sigh on the skin of his neck, her breath warm and scented with chocolate. "Did you threaten him? Tell the truth."

"Not in the least but I'm pretty sure he wanted to clock me. I did tell him that wouldn't be wise."

"That's the truth. You had at least four inches and sixty pounds on him, not that I haven't seen you tangle with someone bigger than you and win. I suppose I should thank you for defending my honor."

He let his hand slip from her cheek all the way down to the small of her back where he splayed his fingers and pulled her closer. Her eyes grew wide and her lips parted in surprise but she didn't protest or try to tug away.

All be damned.

"You don't have to thank me, princess. It was purely my pleasure." His phone vibrated in his pocket. "Sorry, I need to see who this is. I'm expecting a call from Jason."

He stepped back to answer and saw Wyatt's name displayed on the screen. Swiping his thumb, he lifted the phone to his ear and prayed the man had good news for Arden.

"Wyatt, how's it going?"

There was music in the background as if he was in a bar or nightclub. "Not bad. I wanted to check in with you and let you know what's going on."

"Any leads?"

The sound of a door opening and then the music stopped. Wyatt must have stepped outside wherever he was. "Sorry about that racket. I was meeting an informant but he never showed. That's one of the two things I wanted to talk to you about. I have a few leads on Cavendish's whereabouts but nothing concrete. I think he's in Chicago based on some sightings, but he's still using cash so I can't pinpoint his location. Yet. But I will. It's only a matter of time."

Wyatt had the instincts of a prize bloodhound so Shane had no doubt that the man would succeed. "I appreciate all the work you've put into this. You said that was one of two things. What's the other?"

"Hold on while I get in my car." The sound of a door opening and then slamming shut was heard, then an engine firing up. "I was working on a lead with Jason and he had some information you might want. Since I was calling you anyway, he asked me to give you the particulars. He found the detective that worked on Susannah Hollis's murder investigation."

That was great news. The case file had been a joke. "That's terrific. Where does he live and I'll go talk to him."

"The last address he found was in Plainfield, just outside of Indianapolis. I'll text it to you. I hope he can help."

"I hope so too. Thanks for passing that on. I think I'll go talk to him tomorrow."

"I need to get back to work. I'll call when I know more."

Shane hung up and slipped his phone back in his pocket, giving Arden a smile. "Good news. Wyatt's connections have sightings of your father in Chicago. That means he's alive and well, at least for now. We're closing in on him."

Tears sparkled in her eyes and her fingers pressed against her lips. "Thank God. I've been so worried, Shane, and honestly I really still am. He's into something bad and I don't think he's safe."

"I can't argue that but let's hold on to the good news part. He's alive right now but he's still using cash, so he is determined to stay under the radar."

"I'm scared," Arden whispered. "After everything I've learned since he left, I need my dad more than ever."

Shane didn't even hesitate, drawing her back into his arms. She laid her head on his chest while his fingers played with a few silky curls at the nape of her neck. "We're doing everything we can to find him and get him back to you safely."

"I'm angry with him." Her voice was soft and he barely heard her over the cicadas chirping in the background. "I'm so mad that he kept all of this from me and then when I need him the most he's gone. I'm not sure how much longer I can hold myself together and act normal."

"You're doing awesome, just amazing. I just need you to hang in there a little while longer." He tipped her chin up so he was looking into her eyes. "You can always lean on me. I'll be here for you no matter what."

Her chin quivered and her arms tightened around his middle. "I can't expect that of you."

She meant because of their past but all Shane could think about was this moment, right now. He had the woman he loved in his arms and every instinct inside of him had welled up to protect her with everything he had, even if it meant giving up his own life.

"I'd be a real bastard if I left you to deal with all of this yourself. My mother raised her sons better than that, Arden."

Their gazes clashed and something hot and elemental passed between them so quickly he might have thought he imagined it. But no. It had been there. She might not still love him but she still wanted him. There had been remembrance in her eyes, and he knew without a doubt she was thinking about all the nights they'd lain in the back of his truck looking up at the stars under a homemade quilt.

Naked as the day they were born.

His heart accelerated under her palms when she didn't drag

her gaze away, instead looking at him boldly. "I always liked your mother. She was sweet to me."

"She liked you."

The moment seemed to stretch on forever and the rest of the world was forgotten until reality reared its ugly head and Aunt Lydia bustled onto the patio, throwing up her hands.

"There you are! I've been looking all over for you. There are some people I want you to meet. They were friends of your mother, Arden."

They both stepped back and Shane instantly felt the loss of warmth from her body. Arden smiled at her aunt but the sideways glance she gave Shane looked wistful. He was sure he was imagining it. It had been a moment but it was over and she was probably glad.

He, on the other hand, wouldn't sleep a wink tonight.

Chapter Seventeen

"DON'T TAKE ME back to the hotel. Not yet. Take me somewhere. Take me anywhere."

Arden had spoken those words when the party was over and before they left for Indianapolis. The fact was she felt restless and it was because of this man next to her. He'd held her in his arms, touched her, comforted her and it had been as close to heaven as she could possibly get here on earth.

She'd never forgotten how good his body felt pressed so closely to hers, but the memory had dulled over the years apparently because with one touch he'd awoken a million little nerve endings in her flesh and they all craved one thing.

Shane.

Keeping her distance hadn't worked. Then trying to be strictly friends wasn't succeeding either. This wasn't even about the past anymore, which shocked her the most. This was about the man he'd become. Shane was strong, caring, protective, funny, and smart and she'd fallen in love with him all over again, but this time as a grown woman. It made her feelings for him then seem small in comparison.

It was madness, of course. But she simply wanted what little she could have of him while they were together. Soon her father would be found and she'd be back to her old life. Shane would go off with the latest in a long line of gorgeous Barbie dolls and all she'd have was her memories to keep her warm at night. So she might as well make them good because they'd have to last a hell of a long time.

Now they were racing down a dark street on the outskirts of Hemingdale on the back of a borrowed motorcycle. Shane had seen one of the caterers dismount from an older model bike when they'd arrived and after her declaration had gone back inside the party to hunt him down. Much to the man's astonishment, Shane offered him a large sum of money for a short term "rental" of the bike. He hadn't believed it at first but when Shane assured him he was serious and showed him the cash, the younger man had been more than happy to make a quick buck. Especially after Lydia assured him that Shane could be trusted.

Thankfully it was a warm and humid night, summer's last hurrah here in the middle of the country. Arden had laughingly hiked up her dress and thrown her leg over the seat, thrilled that they were going for a ride. There was nothing like the hum of the engine between her legs or the way Shane's muscled back felt against her front, her arms wrapped around him tightly. Their bodies moved in concert with each dip and turn until he finally brought the motorcycle to a halt in a grove of trees far from the lights of the little town.

A small stream gurgled nearby and a few crickets chirped, but otherwise there was silence all around them as if they were the only two people on the planet. Much like earlier, but this time the tension was strung even tighter after their ride and her legs were shaking as he helped her off the bike.

Her high heels sunk into the soft ground as she stood in front of him, not wanting any excess distance between them. She could smell the tang of aftershave and the hint of clean sweat mixed with the aroma of earth and night sky.

"Thank you."

There wasn't anyone for miles, but she whispered anyway not wanting to disturb this fragile peace between them. One wrong move and they'd be back where they'd started that night at the charity party that felt so long ago but had really only been a few weeks. So much had happened, but mostly her heart had overruled her head time and again.

Even now it pounded against her sternum as she struggled to take in her next breath. Their gazes were locked and she could swear she'd seen that look in his eyes before, but it was probably all just a fantasy her mind had conjured up out of the twinkling stars. A bit of make-believe romance to make herself feel better about falling so far and so fast for him.

Again.

She'd been a goner that summer fifteen years ago, practically love at first sight. He'd been the sexier than sin older guy at a picnic and she'd been dazzled from the moment he'd said hello, that dimple in his cheek showing. How she'd ever found the strength to leave him in the end she didn't know, but perhaps that girl had been wiser than the grown woman.

"You're welcome. Are you okay? Do you want to talk?"

The last thing she wanted to do was talk. Highly overrated, it wouldn't fix the hole that had been in her heart since the day she'd left. It wouldn't bring back her blissful ignorance of her family's past.

And it sure wouldn't erase the reason she'd left him to go away.

But there was one thing he could do to stop the pain, if only for a little while. It was a band-aid on a broken limb, but what was a woman in love to do at a moment like this? The woman she'd become might walk away and worry about her dignity but the girl she'd been?

Grab onto all she could get with two greedy hands.

"No, I don't want to talk. I want…"

"Yes?" Shane moved closer, his body radiating heat and she pressed her hands to his chest. "What do you want, my princess?"

Her lips parted to say it but fear clutched at her chest. If he turned her away, she'd crawl away and die.

Her mouth was dry and she licked her lips, her voice shaking with desire and terror, all at the same time.

"I…I need…"

His gaze softened and his fingers traced her jaw before caressing her mouth. Her breath escaped in one painful exhale as her tongue lapped at his thumb. His other arm yanked her against the hard planes of his body, the heat of his flesh searing through the thin material of her cocktail dress but she welcomed the burn.

It had been so long. Too long.

Shane bent his head and buried his face in her neck, his voice rumbling in her ear. "Tell me what you want."

Arden's throat was tight but she managed to croak out one word. "You."

It was enough.

His mouth came down on hers hot and urgent as his callused hands plucked at the zipper on the back of her dress, tugging it down so the material fell off her shoulders and pooled at her waist. The sound of his groan tightened the coil in her lower abdomen and ratcheted up her arousal level almost instantly.

The bulge in his slacks told of his own want and need and she reached down to cup him through the fabric. He felt hot and hard, seeming to grow beneath her fingers and she rubbed his length until he was gasping with pleasure. If she only had tonight, she wanted to give him everything.

Reluctantly, he pulled back with a grimace. "Easy, honey. We don't want this to be over before it starts. I've got a lot of plans for you. Every inch of you, in fact."

She shivered at the promise in his words and was rewarded with another soul-searing kiss that curled her toes and took her breath away. His deft fingers, far too skilled with ladies' lingerie, made quick work of the clasp on the back of her bra and she felt it slide down her arms. The night air tightened her nipples and she moaned in pleasure when his tongue rasped over an already pebbled bud.

Her knees gave way and he caught her easily, lifting her onto the seat of the motorcycle, the leather cool on her overheated skin. Facing her, Shane insinuated himself between her thighs as her skirt tangled around her hips, urging her legs to wrap around his waist. She braced her hands behind her and leaned back to give him better access and he immediately took advantage of her bowed torso, capturing a hard nipple between his lips and scraping it with his tongue.

Pleasure surged through her veins like a fire on the prairie, leaving her panting and wild, her nails digging into his wide shoulders. The untamable need to have him closer, pressed against her own flesh was overwhelming and she groaned his name, a plea for mercy on her tongue. The ache between her legs was almost unbearable and only Shane deep inside of her would ease the pain. She'd fantasized about this so many times but the reality was more, much more.

"I know what you need. Don't worry, I'll make sure you get it."

Dropping to his knees on the carpet of grass, Shane hooked his fingers in the waistband of her panties. She felt a tug and then the sound of tearing fabric as a breeze ran over her now bare slit. He tossed her legs over his shoulders and pressed first one finger and then another inside her, so wet they slid in easily. Hooking his fingers, he unerringly found that sweet spot deep inside her that had her keening his name and clenching his head with her thighs.

Clutching the back of his head, she let her lids flutter shut as his tongue flicked over her swollen clit and a shudder of intense pleasure ran through her frame. He drew a whimper from her lips as he lapped at the pearl while his fingers pumped in and out of her slick channel. White hot flames built inside of her until all she could do was say his name over and over again, her body shaking with the force of not just pleasure but pure emotion.

This was the man she loved.

"Come for me."

Such a simple request but he still held sway over her body even after all this time. She cried out as her pleasure crested and then rolled over her as bright-hot lights danced behind her lids. She was trembling and tried to gather herself, but Shane didn't allow that for a second. She heard the telltale sound of a zipper and the press of his hot, hard length against her thigh.

"Is it safe? I'm clean," he rasped, his voice deep and dark. It sent a tingle down her spine and she nodded, giving him the permission he sought.

"Yes. Please."

Pushing into her, Shane's length seemed to drive the oxygen from her lungs. Her breathing ragged, she bit her lip as he stretched her far past anything she'd had since their last time. He filled her completely and totally, owning her in a way no one else ever had or ever would. She belonged to him body and soul.

His hands grasped her hips and he lifted her up so he could straddle the bike before settling onto the seat with her impaled deeply on his shaft.

"Fuck, baby. You feel so hot and tight. Ride me."

She didn't bother telling him she was tight because she hadn't been with a man in a few years. Her marriage hadn't been the most passionate and at the end it hadn't been physical at all. She hadn't mourned the loss of it until she'd seen Shane again, the bad boy waking up her dormant libido and making her remember all the naughty things they used to do to one another.

Still wearing her high heels, she wrapped her legs around him as he used his considerable strength to lift her up and then down, his length rubbing delicious spots inside and sending her closer to release once again. She leaned back until her spine touched the bike as Shane pounded into her, his feet braced on the ground and his hands on her ample bottom. She'd have a few small bruises tomorrow but what a lovely reminder of their shared passion.

Teetering on the very edge of the cliff, Arden's hand slid down her belly to the swollen button between her legs but Shane chuckled and slapped it away.

"That's my job, baby girl. Are you ready to come for me?" His thumb brushed the nub over and over until her body was strung tight as a bow. "Come hard. I want you to scream my name so everyone knows where you get your pleasure."

His name was on her lips when her release exploded in her abdomen and radiated out to her extremities like waves lapping at the shore, pulling and pushing until she was wrung out and breathless.

Shane's own head was thrown back, the cords of his neck in stark relief as he found his own climax. She watched fascinated as a muscle worked in his jaw but his gaze never wavered from her own. It was hot, sexy, and incredibly beautiful to witness.

When they were done, he pulled her into his arms so they were skin to skin, his face buried in her hair. They didn't move for a long time until eventually she felt him pull away slightly, a warm breeze caressing her damp flesh.

"That was worth the wait. How about we head back to the hotel and do it again?"

There were a million reasons to refuse and only one to say yes, so of course she nodded her head in agreement.

She'd think about the consequences tomorrow.

✦   ✦   ✦

SHANE'S LIDS OPENED halfway, checking the digital clock on the nightstand. It was just after five in the morning and still dark outside the heavy drapes in their hotel room. He'd fallen asleep only a few hours ago but he wasn't complaining. He also wasn't unhappy in the least about the warm, womanly form draped over him, her breasts pressed to his chest and her head cradled on his shoulder.

He was still in something of a daze. Arden had expressed her need for him last night and he hadn't hesitated to make love to her, even in an unusual locale such as on a bike seat in the woods. Afterwards, he'd returned the motorcycle to its owner and driven her back here, where they'd proceeded to try out shower sex for the first time.

Clean and sated, they'd gone to sleep but now that he was awake he was finding that *all* parts of him were awake. He couldn't wait another minute to be with the woman he loved. Who needed food and sleep when he had this unbelievable happiness filling every nook and cranny inside of him and making his heart almost burst out of his chest?

He'd been given a precious second chance with the most important person in his world.

They'd been apart so long he didn't want to waste a moment now that they were back together. In fact, he had a fun idea as to how to wake her up for a little pre-dawn romp.

Sliding under the covers, he gently rolled Arden onto her back and positioned himself between her legs. He pressed kisses onto the sensitive flesh behind her knee and then up toward the apex of her thighs, nipping and licking along the way.

Arden's hips twitched and jerked and a soft moan escaped from her lips but her limbs were still heavy with sleep. Running his tongue along the folds of her slit, he pressed a finger in her already dripping channel, the walls hugging his digit tightly.

"Shane."

He lifted the covers to take a peek and Arden's eyes were closed but the lids were beginning to flutter with wakefulness. He bent his head again, getting back to work and lapped at her swollen button until her fingers twisted in his hair and his name was being groaned in a sleepy tone.

"Good morning, princess," he said against her most private place, blowing a breath over her clit and feeling her tremble in response. Her legs moved restlessly and she tugged at his hair until he slid up her body.

"It's not morning," she mumbled crossly, although her hips were grinding against his so she didn't seem to mind the early wake up call. "The sun isn't even up. You're evil, Shane Anderson."

Shane grinned wickedly as he ran a fingertip around an already pebbled nipple. "It's morning somewhere in the world, but if you want me to I'll let you go back to sleep."

Arden snorted, not in the least delicate or ladylike but he loved the fire in her so much it made him ache. "You woke me up, you better finish this."

"Your wish is my command."

She was so wet he slid in easily all the way to the hilt and he sucked in a breath as she surrounded him, hot and snug. He started up a slow, rocking rhythm, savoring every moment of being one with her and in no hurry to end it even as he felt that familiar tingle in his lower back and a flush on his neck.

Burying his face in the fragrant curve of her neck, he groaned as she wrapped her legs around his waist, her heels digging into his ass as they moved in perfect synchronicity, their bodies acting as one entity. Her nails scraped his shoulders and that primal voice inside of him chanted in his ear, drowning out their ragged breathing and the slap of skin on skin.

Deeper. Harder. Faster.

He lifted her knees on his elbows so he could drive into her very core and that's when the flutters of her climax began, the walls clenching as he thrust into her again and again. Her orgasm tore his own release from him; his balls pulled up painfully to his body as it turned him inside out and left him exhausted and reeling. Nothing felt as good as being with Arden. How had he gone so long without *her*, without *this*? When she'd left he must have become used to walking around without his heart.

He rolled onto his back and carried her with him, tucking her into his body with his arms wrapped around her. Her skin was soft under his fingertips and he stroked down her arm, delighting in her shivers and giggles as she fell back asleep.

Shane felt sleep overcome him as well and he gave into the fatigue knowing the morning would bring a new day, but this time he wouldn't be alone anymore. Their future started now.

Chapter Eighteen

ARDEN COULD FEEL the change in the air when they awoke and began to get ready for their day. Shane was singing in the shower at the top of his lungs a song from that summer so long ago. It had been playing that first day when they met at the picnic on the lake. Before he'd stepped into the bathroom, he'd even grinned and given her a long, slow kiss.

The kiss wasn't the kind from a man who had a one night stand with an old flame. The kind a handsome, popular bachelor gave a female the next morning to say he'd had a great time but there was no future.

No, this kiss held promise. It was all about love and commitment and forever.

Holy shit, what had she done?

There could never be a forever for the two of them. The reason she'd left him hadn't gone away although her love had never died. It had never occurred to her – idiot that she was – that perhaps his hadn't either. She'd been too lost in her own pain to notice if he was hurting too. Now she was going to have to shoot him down once again. She had no choice.

She loved him so very much and wanted only the best for

him. His happiness was miles more important than her own. She could only hope he would forgive her someday, although she wouldn't be forgiving herself for last night. Not ever. It had been weak and indulgent and she despised herself for what she'd done and was going to have to do.

"Do you want to go somewhere for breakfast or order room service?" Shane asked when he joined her in the main room. He'd put on a pair of blue jeans and a white button down shirt, the seams straining at his wide shoulders.

She was about to take the light out of his beautiful green eyes and she hated herself for it.

"Actually, I have a few things to do this morning. I was thinking about just grabbing a muffin and coffee on the way."

She began gathering up her sunglasses and room key, stuffing them into her purse. She heard Shane moving behind her and then he was standing right next to her, his fingers twirling one of her still damp curls. "That's fine with me. What are we doing today? Just remember that we need to check on that detective that worked your mother's case."

Licking her suddenly dry lips, she zipped her bag closed, keeping her gaze studiously away from his. "Why don't you do that and I'll go run my errands?"

His warm chuckle sent shivers down her spine and her body stiffened when he pulled her into his arms. "Why would we do that separately, sweetheart? I don't mind taking you where you need to go. If you want to do some shopping, hell, I'll even hold your packages."

Tears pricked the back of her eyes and a pain sliced through her heart, but then she deserved it. If she could take all his pain away and bear it herself she would in a second with no hesitation. "I thought I'd go by myself."

Her choked words along with her rigid posture must have tipped him off that all was not right in the world. He slowly let her go, dropping his arms to his side and stepped back, regarding her steadily.

"Jesus, I'm so fucking dumb." He walked over to the windows, his jaw tight and his expression pained. "Say it."

"Shane—"

"Say it, goddammit," he snarled, whirling on the heel of his boot, his eyes blazing with anger. "Don't wimp out on me now. Fucking say it."

The words "I love you. I want to spend the rest of my life with you" were right on the tip of her tongue but somehow she wrestled those feelings to the ground even as she ripped her own heart out of her chest. She didn't have the luxury of thinking about herself.

"Last night…" she began, watching as his fury turned to anguish. She had to push every word out through a lump the size of Texas in her throat. "Last night was wonderful and amazing but we can't continue this. We're grown adults now and what we had was over long ago. We have our own lives."

"You are such a liar. I know you felt what I felt last night and this morning. I'm not some naive kid anymore, baby. I'm a grown ass man that knows when a woman feels more than just a great orgasm. But for some reason you're bound and determined to pretend that you don't feel a thing and for the life of me I can't understand why. What are you so afraid of? Is it me? I know I've sown some wild oats but that's because you left. It's all in the past now."

He looked almost hopeful and she couldn't let him have even a glimmer of it. It would be too cruel. "I'm not lying. Last night was a mistake."

Arden was shocked that lightning didn't strike her dead. From the angrily amused look on Shane's face she hadn't convinced him of her sincerity.

"You're right, honey. Last night was a mistake and I made it." He moved closer so she could feel his warm breath on her face and smell the clean scent of his body wash. Her fingers yearned to reach out and touch him and she had to curl her hands into fists, the nails digging into her palms to stop herself. "We should have cleared the air about the past before I allowed us to make love again. But it's not too late. We can do it right now."

No, no, no. This wasn't any better. Talking about the past wasn't good.

"What did you have in mind?"

Her question was a delay tactic. She knew good and well what he wanted to know.

"I think we should start with the summer we dated and go from there. I imagine we have quite a bit of ground to cover. I'll order us some breakfast. You might want to get comfortable. I think we'll be here for a while."

Her mind whirled with possibilities and they all ended up with her running out of the door, which was ridiculous. He'd catch her before her hand was on the lever. From the determined look on his face, he'd follow her to the ends of the earth to get his answers.

Dammit, she'd never wanted him to know but he wasn't giving her many options. He was right, she was a terrible liar and she didn't have one handy that would answer his burning question. Sinking down on the sofa, she waited while he ordered breakfast. Her brain was still in denial that she was actually going to have to tell him the truth. Even her best friend back in New York didn't know. It was private and painful and she was going to have to find the words to tell him.

Sitting down on a chair to her right, he stretched out his long legs and handed her one of the two cups of coffee he'd poured from the bar in the corner of the room. "I guess I'll start since you look like you're about to run for the far hills. I'm pissed that you didn't tell me you were leaving. I thought we meant more to each other than that, Arden. Of course your daddy made sure to shatter any notions I might have had that you cared for me. He said you were happy to be moving on and glad to see me in your rearview mirror."

Arden could hear her own heart pounding in her ears, heavy and growing ever louder. He'd cut to the quick, but then she'd hurt him badly and she didn't blame him for hating her. She'd expected it, although seeing his green eyes filled with distrust instead of love was more painful than she'd imagined.

Swallowing the lump lodged in her throat, she tried to find the words to express emotions that even now she wasn't sure she understood. "We did mean a lot to each other."

His eyes narrowed, appraising her from head to toe but not in a tender fashion. This was something different, something colder. He was trying to decide if she was lying.

"Then why did you go?"

"We always knew I had to go back to school, Shane. It was always the plan. You had to go back to school too."

He wasn't buying what she was selling.

"Yes, at the end of August. You left three weeks early. Why?"

She was holding the cup so tightly her knuckles were white. Loosening her fingers, she took a few deep breaths as she tried to find an answer that would satisfy him.

"It was time," she said softly, avoiding his gaze that saw way too much. "It was time for me to go."

He didn't say a word. He simply sat there, his brows raised waiting for her to continue. She fought the urge to speak more but she knew she'd lose. A few minutes later, she broke.

"Dammit, Shane. What do you expect me to say? Better yet, why did you expect me to stay? What would have happened if I had?" Too nervous to stay still, she hopped to her feet, her arms wrapped protectively around her torso. She was shaking with anger, plus a whole lot of remembered hurt. And love. The memories of how they loved each other had never died. "Were we going to get married and live happily ever after? Were the Andersons and Cavendishs going to bury the hatchet and have picnics in the park while you and I produced grandchildren for them to dote on? Was there a dog and picket fence in this scenario too? Were you honestly going to give up your playboy ways and settle down with me, Shane? Be faithful with one woman for the rest of your life? Could you even do it?"

Arden grabbed a tissue from the bar and dabbed at her runny nose and teary eyes. She'd sworn not to become emotional over all of this again but here she was, blubbering like it all happened yesterday.

"Yes."

Whirling around, her gaze locked onto Shane, still in his chair but he was now sitting up straight, his shoulders tense.

"Yes," he repeated, a white ring around his lips.

Shaking her head, she sagged against the bar, the bile in her stomach threatening to make an appearance. "I don't understand what you mean."

Slowly he stood, towering over her, his gaze never wavering. "I said yes. Yes, I wanted to marry you. Yes, I wanted our families to bury the hatchet. Yes, I wanted to have a family, and a dog, and a goddamn picket fence with you. Yes, I wanted to settle down and yes, I planned on being faithful for the rest of my damn life with you. And do you know why, Arden?"

He was standing so close now she could smell his aftershave and feel the heat from his body. Her legs grew weak and she had to grab onto the counter for support as she stared helplessly into his green eyes that at the moment were almost black with emotion.

"Because I fucking love you. So yes, I planned on all those things. I thought you did too. It's what we talked about."

She gathered up the shreds of her courage and stood tall under his scrutiny, despite the urge to double over in agony. Hearing him say he loved her was almost more than she could bear. She'd cherish those words until the day she died. "And that's why I left you."

He frowned, clearly not understanding what she meant. "You left because we planned a future together? That doesn't make any goddamn sense, Arden. Unless of course you didn't love me but this morning leads me to believe you did. Or at least you do now."

All the walls she'd so carefully built around her had fallen to the ground and she stood before him with no defenses. "I did love you and that's why I left. Because that future we planned? With the house and the kids and the dog? That wasn't going to happen. It couldn't happen."

"Why not?" Shane's gaze had softened and she had to look away from the love shining in his eyes. "Because of Ben? Honey, we could have handled your father. Together we could have handled anything."

She shook her head, tears beginning to stream down her face, her throat tight with love and pain. She could taste the salt on her lips and she scrubbed at her cheeks with the back of her hand.

"I left because I was filled with tumors. I left because they thought I might have cancer." She looked up to see the growing horror in his expression. "I left because I knew no matter what happened I wouldn't be able to give you those children. I had a hysterectomy, Shane. They took everything and with it all of our dreams. I left you not because I didn't love you enough, but because I loved you. Too much."

Chapter Nineteen

SHANE'S LEGS WERE numb and he stumbled backwards to sit on the couch, still too shocked to respond. The pain in his chest felt like she'd taken a filleting knife and sliced into the flesh dozens of times. All this time he thought she'd left because she didn't love him after all.

Fuck. Shit.

"Cancer?"

He'd only been able to get out one word, his voice like ground glass. A sweep of fear ran through him and his gaze ran up and down her, looking for any telltale signs that she might still be sick. If she was he'd take her to every specialist in the world to cure whatever disease she might have. He'd spend his last dollar making sure she was healthy.

Arden's hands wrung together and she shook her head. "Luckily it wasn't cancer. But they didn't like the way a growth looked on one of my ovaries and combined with my other issues…"

He swallowed hard and tried to calm himself but he could still hear the pounding of his pulse in his ears. "Other issues? What other issues? Maybe you should start from the beginning."

She moved over to the windows, staring out over the city. "I don't know if you remember but I had really painful and long periods. They were really hard on me and I often had to take to my bed and just sleep through the first day or so."

"Yes, I remember, although I also remember that you tried to play it off as no big deal. But it was, wasn't it?"

How much had she not told him?

She nodded slowly, still not meeting his gaze. "It was. My uterus was filled with fibroid tumors and I was on prescription painkillers for my menstrual cramps. I also had severe endometriosis so they put me on the pill when I was seventeen after surgery to help correct the condition. That helped for a while but eventually the pain came back even worse. I can't tell you how hard it was for me to hide it from you that summer. I was in pain almost constantly and it made it hard to even get out of bed some days. At one point I hoped that everything would be okay and I could come back to you but the first surgery didn't have good news."

Scraping his hand down his face, Shane absorbed what she'd told him. Looking back, he could now see that she'd had good days and bad. Days when she "wasn't in the mood" to make love and other times when she'd been what he would have labeled as "overemotional", but her feisty, zest for life attitude had hidden most of her issues. If she hadn't said anything he never would have guessed.

Which didn't say much for him as a boyfriend. Shit, how self-absorbed had he been to have missed the signs? She must have thought he was a narcissistic idiot and he wouldn't argue with her.

"You never said anything."

She finally turned to look at him, tears in her eyes. "I know. I was a young girl and embarrassed. I'd never been close enough to a guy to talk about, you know, female problems. Plus, I was scared. It felt like I was going every week for ultrasounds and check-ups. That growth on my ovary kept getting bigger and I couldn't keep ignoring the doctor's warnings anymore. Father was beside himself and Grandmother kept telling me to just have the surgery. I didn't know what to do or who to talk to."

"The surgery? They wanted you to have a hysterectomy?"

Shane had to wonder if he'd even known what that was when he was twenty-three. He certainly wouldn't have been able to give her any sort of advice or opinion but he could have held her and told her it was all going to be okay. Not that he would have known whether it would be or not.

"Yes, they'd tried other methods and as I said they didn't like what they saw. But I was so scared. There were aftereffects, not the least of which was that I would never be able to get pregnant. I'd never have your baby, Shane."

Hanging his head, he rubbed the back of his neck more from shame than anything else. Obviously, he'd done a shitty job of showing her how much she meant to him, but then they hadn't had long together. "I wouldn't have cared about that, Arden. The only thing I would have cared about was keeping you healthy and alive. If that meant we didn't have kids, so be it. Nothing means more to me than you do."

A tear slipped down her cheek and landed on her white blouse. "It's easy to say but the reality is much different. I couldn't rob you of your chance to be a father. I couldn't do that to you."

His head jerked up and his brows pulled together. "Easy? You think it's easy to say? That I'm just being glib to spare your feelings? Fuck, Arden." He stood and strode to where she was standing by the window, his fingers clamping down on her arms. "Giving up on the idea of being a dad isn't easy but compared to giving you up? That's not even a contest. You win every time. Hell, we could have adopted or had a surrogate. Or we could have rescued half a dozen dogs and spoiled the hell out of them. It wouldn't have been easy but we would have been together. Dammit, I loved you."

His hands dropped away and he paced the floor, his fingers scraping through his hair. "I know why you didn't tell me but damn, I wish you would have. I wish you could have given me a chance to be more than a stupid, self-centered kid. We lost so many years, princess."

He couldn't stop his own tears now and the last few words came out choked as his throat closed up. Struggling to drag air into his aching chest, he gripped the edge of the bar fighting the urge to smash his knuckles into the polished oak, creating one pain to help alleviate another greater one.

"I had so many emotions to deal with, Shane, but mostly I was scared. Worst case, I had cancer and best case I might not lose all of my female organs but the chances of ever having a baby were low. I was terrified, literally shaking in my shoes every time I went to the doctor. I guess…I guess I just wasn't sure you were ready to make that big of a decision about the rest of your life. The dreams we'd talked about were so different than what I would have asked you to embrace."

It came down to one fact. And it hurt.

"You didn't trust me."

Arden sucked in a breath and he knew he'd hit a bullseye.

"It wasn't like that."

"Wasn't it? You didn't trust me to stand by you when you were sick. You didn't trust that I loved you more than those silly fantasies we had. And you sure as shit didn't trust me with how much pain you were in *every goddamn day* that we were together. In fact, you went you of your way to make sure I didn't know. So don't say it wasn't like that. That's exactly how it was."

She shook her head, her lips trembling as more tears fell. "I wanted the best for you. I was protecting you from settling for a life that you wouldn't be happy with."

"You thought I would come to resent you eventually?" he prompted.

"Yes, and I couldn't stand to see your love grow into hate."

He shrugged and wiped at his damp cheeks with the back of his hand. He was secure enough in his manhood to shed some tears. "I think I need some air, so let's forget about breakfast."

"Where are you going?"

Despite the pain he was in he was still coherent enough to hear the echoing pain in her voice. She was hurting as much as he was but he could barely deal with his own.

"Somewhere. Anywhere. Maybe back to the lake from last night. Maybe to a bar or a strip joint. Hell, maybe I'll hop a flight to Vegas. I just know I need some space."

"I'm so sorry, Shane." Arden choked and she buried her face in her hands, her shoulders shaking with sobs. "I just loved you so much. I never stopped. I swear I've thought about you so many times over the years. I wanted you to be happy even if it wasn't with me."

It was hard to be angry with her for a misguided but selfless act.

He still loved her.

He didn't like her all that much at the moment.

He was angry at what had been stolen from them. Frustrated at thinking that she didn't love him all this time. It had been a waste and he couldn't quite wrap his mind around the consequences – to both of them – from this one decision.

Fifteen years ago, Arden had turned her back on him. This time it was his turn. He grabbed his key card and stuffed it in his pocket, betrayal and hurt churning in his gut and bringing the bile up into his throat.

He walked out of the door.

✦ ✦ ✦

ARDEN'S SOBBING FINALLY subsided sometime after Shane walked out. At first, she'd thought he would immediately turn around and come back but as the minutes ticked away she realized she'd hurt him too much. He was angry and in pain, the same wound that festered in her own heart. Truthfully she wasn't sure how they were supposed to come back from damage this deep.

At some point, their breakfast had arrived and she was sure the waiter was worried she was either a criminal on the run or a rock star as she'd kept her head down so her hair fell over her face. She hadn't wanted him to see her cry.

Padding into the bathroom, she rinsed her face with cool

water and tried to repair her red, swollen eyes. She wasn't a pretty crier and this was worse than usual. Between the black mascara running down her face and the splotchy skin she was officially a mess.

Once put back together she popped open a ginger ale and settled onto the couch, her stomach too queasy to even entertain the idea of eating. Feeling like the world had ended took a lot out of a person.

She didn't blame him for leaving. On the contrary, he'd shown amazing patience and managed to hold onto his temper even when she'd known he was furious.

He was also right. She hadn't trusted him or herself but she'd been not much more than a child at the time, terrified and easily persuaded. Her father had been the first to plant the idea that Shane might not want a female that couldn't give him children. She couldn't blame Ben, however. He might have planted the seed but she'd given it plenty of water and sunlight until it had taken over every thought in her head. She'd been obsessed with Shane turning his back on her either then or in the future.

Listlessly, she checked her phone for any messages before switching on the television. The noise made her feel less alone. But it didn't change the fact that she was.

✦   ✦   ✦

SHANE WALKED ALONG the city streets, hands shoved in the pockets of his jacket and his eyes down. He barely registered the sounds and people around him, his mind focused on one person.

Arden.

It was too late for what-if's, although a torrent of them had run through his mind since he walked out of the hotel room. She hadn't believed in him and that hurt. But she'd been hurting just as badly or worse, going through a nightmare he wouldn't have wished on his worst enemy. He was angry and sad that he hadn't been there and he'd taken it out on her.

What part had Ben played in all this?

He couldn't get that question out of his mind either. Young Arden had idolized her father to the point she hadn't believed a word Shane had said against him. Facts and evidence hadn't made a bit of difference; she'd been loyal and true. If Daddy Dearest pushed her to leave Shane then there was a good chance she would have done just that.

With the unfurling truth about her past, it was clear she'd been lied to and manipulated most of her life. It wasn't a shock that she'd left him. Not really. Sheltered and naive, she would have taken every word from Ben's lips as the truth.

Another reason to kick his ass the next time Shane saw him.

The past couldn't be changed. They were different people than they had been but the feelings were still there, stronger if anything. If they tried hard perhaps they could have a future together. It wouldn't be easy; there was a great deal of hurt to work through, but being with Arden would be worth it.

Stopping suddenly on the sidewalk, Shane smacked his forehead and groaned silently.

What in the hell am I doing here?

They'd been given the thing he'd hoped and prayed for…a second chance. Now he only hoped he hadn't blown it. He turned on his heel and headed straight back to the hotel. And Arden.

Chapter Twenty

THE HOTEL DOOR was thrown open and Shane stood in the opening with an intense expression on his handsome face. Arden's heart lurched in her chest and her breath halted for a moment as her scrambled brain tried to make sense of what was about to happen. Was he here to scream and yell? Tell her she was a terrible person? Pack his things and leave?

He strode in and stood in front of her as she huddled on the couch, her knees brought up to her chest and her arms wrapped around her legs protectively.

"I'm sorry. I'm a fucking idiot but I'm sorry. Please forgive me."

Huh?

"What? I don't understand."

"I'm sorry," he repeated, the words echoing in her head. "Please forgive me."

Letting go of her legs, Arden stood up on trembling knees. "What exactly am I forgiving you for?"

A smile slowly blossomed on his face, showing off the Anderson dimple in his cheek. "For being stupid and walking out. I should have got down on my knees and thanked the heavens that you loved me that much then and maybe still do, but I had to get all butthurt and bent out of shape. Can you forgive me?"

He still loved her. He was talking about a future and that's what she wanted, so why was she hesitating?

There was one thing they needed to clear up. He had to understand.

"I can't have children, Shane. Can you be okay with that? I made peace with it years ago but I know this is a shock to you."

"I can be. I guess you'll just have to get all my love and attention. You won't have to share me." His expression turned serious, his brow wrinkled. "I know we have a lot of work to do here and I'm not trying to minimize that. But dammit, I want a second chance. I've never stopped loving you. When I saw you that night at the party, it was like someone had punched me in the gut then gave me an uppercut to the jaw. You make me crazy but mostly you make me happy. Do I make you happy?"

Joy fluttered inside of her like the wings of a thousand butterflies. She'd never believed she'd hear those words again.

"Yes," she whispered, the beating of her heart sounding like a marching band in a Fourth of July parade. "Yes, so much."

"And do you forgive me?" he persisted when all Arden wanted was for him to throw her on the bed and ravish her at least a couple of times.

"Yes, I do. Do you forgive me?"

He shook his head, this time reaching out so his hands ran down her arms before pulling her close. The heat from his body instantly warmed her own and she breathed deeply, letting herself get high on his scent.

"There's nothing to forgive. You were just trying to do the

right thing out of love."

He bent his head so his lips could ghost over hers, softly and then firmer, his tongue snaking out to trace her lower lip.

"I don't know about you but all this forgiveness has worn me out," she said huskily. "Maybe we should lie down for a while."

Before she could take another breath, he'd bent over and pressed a shoulder into her middle so he could carry her, fireman style, back to the bed. Forgiveness was sweet indeed and she intended to savor every moment of it.

✦   ✦   ✦

SHANE PULLED THE rental car into the shaded driveway and peered at the numbers on the house. "This is it. Are you ready? Let's hope this guy has some more information than that flimsy case file."

After a morning of lying in bed and getting much more well-acquainted with one another's bodies, they'd pried themselves out of the hotel room and driven to a town just outside of Indianapolis to see the detective that had worked the Susannah Hollis murder case in Hemingdale. He was now retired and from what Jason could find out the man was also in ill health. Hopefully he might remember something that could help.

Arden caught his hand in hers and smiled. "I'm nervous but I'm not sure why. Maybe it's because he was there that night. That's so…personal."

Shane squeezed her hand as he rang the doorbell. "He was just doing his job. I'm sure he was very professional."

The door swung open and a woman about Shane's age was there greeting them with a smile. "Can I help you?"

Knowing Arden would tease him about it later, Shane turned on the charm hoping she wouldn't slam the door on their faces. They hadn't called ahead of time, as Shane was afraid the detective would refuse to see them. Cops could be strange about their former cases, especially those that were unsolved.

"My name is Shane Anderson and this is Arden Cavendish. We were wondering if perhaps we could speak with Robert Destin?"

The woman's brows pulled together but she nodded. "Hold on here for a moment while I see if Dad is up to having visitors. We're not selling anything."

Shane heard the rumble of an older man's voice and then the door opened again. "You can talk to him but just for a few minutes."

"That's fine," Shane assured her. "This shouldn't take long."

Especially if the detective didn't remember anything or refused to discuss the case. Shane would then simply hand him a business card, thank him for his time, and usher Arden back to the rental car.

They were quickly ensconced on the sofa across from Destin, the gray-haired man sitting in a recliner that had seen better days. His eyes were narrowed in suspicion as he waited for one of them to speak.

Shane cleared this throat and introduced themselves before cutting to the chase. "Detective Destin, we're here about the Susannah Hollis murder. You were the lead on that case, I believe?"

A growl came from deep in the man's chest and he waved his arm in the air as if swatting a fly. "I'm not a cop anymore so you can quit with the detective stuff. My name's Bob and you can call me that. What do you want to know about the Hollis case? That was over thirty years ago."

Shane leaned forward, his elbows on his knees. He and Arden had agreed that he would take the first crack at persuading Destin to talk to them. "I realize it was a long time ago but we were hoping you might remember something that wasn't in the police file. There wasn't much there, to be honest."

Bob leaned back, his gaze darting between Shane and Arden. "What does this have to do with you? Why do you care?"

Her hand came to rest on Shane's thigh. "I'm Arden, Susannah's daughter. I want to know who killed my mother, Mr. Destin. I need to know."

Bob's eyes widened in surprise and his fingers rubbed at his chin before answering. "If you're asking me what I can prove then I have no idea. If you're asking who I believe did it then, young lady, you need look no further than your own father."

Chapter Twenty-One

A SMALL WHILE later, Arden and Shane found themselves in Bob's basement office. He'd kept copies of every case he'd worked on and the walls were lined with file folders.

"When I was younger I thought I might write a book some-day about all my cases, but I let go of that dream a few years ago. I'm no writer. Heck, I don't even like being on my computer if you want to know the truth." The older man grimaced as he pulled the dusty folder from a stack and laid it on the table between Shane and Arden. "I'm sorry about earlier, my dear. My speed bump of judgment seems to be out of order now that I've retired. I shouldn't have said that about your old man."

Arden had been shocked when Destin had declared his opinion, but deep down she'd known Ben had a motive after talking to Delilah.

"It's okay. We asked you and you told us. I want to know who really did it and if it's my father...well...then I'll deal with it. But I thought he was out of town at the time."

Bob sat in the chair across from them. "So did we, but that was before 9/11. It would have been easy to buy a ticket under an assumed name and travel back to Hemingdale, do the deed, and then travel back to St. Louis. His last meeting was at four, which gave him plenty of time to get to Indianapolis. He had motive and opportunity. Statistically speaking, the most dangerous person in a woman's life is the man in her life."

"What about David Hollis? There are witnesses that put him at the scene of the crime," Shane pointed out.

The detective nodded and opened the folder, pulling out two photos. "There was one witness who said they saw him there and three others who said they didn't see anyone. But if you look at Ben and David, they looked so much alike that in dim lighting they could have been mistaken for one another."

Arden held up the two pictures and was struck by their resemblance when they were younger. "David had an alibi?"

"Several witnesses saw him at the local watering hole, and trust me, they knew him well there. He was a regular so they weren't going to confuse him with someone else. Besides, I questioned David Hollis myself. That man was devastated about Susannah's death, just tore up. It was like he was the husband and Ben was the brother-in-law. Ben barely betrayed any emotion even when we questioned him hard. That was one stone cold bastard. It was like it was any other day."

Shane cleared his throat. "Lack of emotion doesn't make him a killer. I'm sure he was busy worrying about Arden and trying to hold things together for her."

Bob shook his head, his lips twisted. "Actually, her grandmother was taking care of her. That woman is a force of nature and she managed to organize the funeral and take care of the baby all at the same time."

As upset as Arden was with her grandmother at the moment,

she couldn't help but smile.

"That sounds like my grandmother. She's a formidable woman."

"She is." Bob stood and shoved his hands into his pockets, shifting his weight from foot to foot. "There are some disturbing crime scene photos in here you might not want to see, Arden. Plus the autopsy report was graphic as well."

Shane frowned and began to page through the file. "Those weren't in the case file at the station."

"They might have been lost, I suppose." The detective rubbed his chin. "Once folders are put in storage things have a way of disappearing. They might have been shoved in the wrong file folder. I doubt they're really gone."

A photo fluttered from the folder and landed in front of Arden. It was a picture of a bedroom with a huge bloodstain on the floor. Shit, these were gruesome and she hadn't even seen an image of her mother, just the scene. Shane snatched it away quickly and turned it face down on the table.

"I suppose that could have happened," Shane conceded. "We're damn lucky you kept copies. Does the police know about your private file collection?"

Bob chuckled and shook his head. "No, and I'd like to keep it that way. Now if you don't mind I'll go on upstairs while you look through this. If you have any questions don't hesitate to ask, but with photos and reports this sensitive and personal it seems like I should leave you both alone. Will you be all right?"

"We will," Arden assured him, relieved she wouldn't have to try and keep up a strong facade in front of the retired officer. "I want to thank you again for this. You can't know how much this means to me."

"I think I might have an idea. Call me if you need me."

Destin headed upstairs and Shane held up the file. "Maybe I should look through this first and weed out anything that might upset you."

Swallowing hard, Arden shook her head. "I've already had a few shocks to my system and I've survived. I need to do this."

She reached for the folder but Shane still held it out of her grasp. "How about we make a deal? You don't look at the crime scene photos but the autopsy report is okay. It will be graphic enough, I think."

Arden chewed on her lower lip and then nodded in agreement. "Deal. Go ahead and pull the photos from the file."

He shuffled the papers and separated the pictures before handing her the folder. She spent the next half hour reading through witness statements that hadn't been in the original file, plus statements from her Uncle David and her father. Both men claimed to have loved her mother and that they would never hurt her in any way.

But in all probability, one of them shot her.

From the police notes, the idea of a random stranger shooting her mother had been discarded rather early in the investigation. The town was small and there had been no rash of violence or even a string of home break-ins or assaults. Plus, the shooting just happened to have occurred when her father was "supposedly" out of town. It pointed to someone who knew Susannah Hollis.

Feeling slightly sick to her stomach after reading the accounts, Arden picked up the autopsy report, her hands shaking slightly. She steeled herself for the gruesome facts of the damage done to her mother's body that night. Luckily the report turned out to be just that...facts. Cold and unemotional, the coroner had recorded the size of the gunshot wound and the damage to her vital organs. Death had been blessedly quick.

Frowning, Arden read through the test reports regarding her mother's blood alcohol level, which had been just below the current legal limit. "This can't be right, Shane. The coroner got this wrong."

He leaned over her shoulder to peer at the documents. "That she had a few drinks that night? She was about your size so I bet she only had to have a couple to feel pretty tipsy."

Arden shook her head and tapped on the paper. "No...this. It says her blood type is O positive. It can't be."

"That's the most common blood type in the world. I'm O positive."

He wasn't getting it. "So is my dad. But I'm A positive. I always assumed my mother was too. I mean...she has to be, right?"

Her fingers clutched the report as a horrible truth took root in her brain. She stared down at the paper, willing the typewritten words to change but they stayed stubbornly the same.

"One of them isn't my parent," she whispered, the bile rising in her throat. She was getting damn tired of finding out secrets in the worst way. Apparently everyone had been lying to her about everything. At this point, what was the truth?

Shane scraped a hand down his face before grabbing onto her hand. "You're the picture of your mother. Everyone can see the resemblance."

A cold numbness was beginning to spread through her body and she welcomed it wholeheartedly. She needed to step away from her emotions to be able to deal with this revelation.

"Then Ben Cavendish isn't my father."

Jumping up from his chair, Shane rubbed the back of his neck as he paced the small space.

"You look like your father a little bit too. Maybe the coroner made a mistake, baby girl."

She picked up another piece of paper. "The blood type is on two different reports, not just the autopsy. The crime scene unit also typed the blood as O positive. I didn't catch it until I saw the autopsy though. It's not a mistake, but I might be."

"Don't say that." His hands rested on her shoulders, trying to reassure her. "Maybe you have your father's blood type wrong."

If only.

"I don't. He used to donate blood quite a bit and there is a plaque on his office wall. O positive."

Arden's nerveless fingers picked up the photo of David Hollis. "Do I look like him? Is he my father? My real father?"

Shane sat down next to her, scooting his chair close so he could pull her into his arms. "I don't know, honey. But this just tells me that it's more important than ever to not only find your father—we also need to find your uncle too."

She dropped the picture onto the table, her hands trembling too much to hold on. "It tells us something more. It tells us that whether David is my father or not…my dad had a more powerful motive than money to kill my mother."

Nothing was ever going to be the same.

Chapter Twenty-Two

SHANE SLID THE keycard into the slot and then pushed open the hotel room door, the aroma of cleaning products hitting his nostrils. When they'd returned to Indianapolis, Jason had called with David Hollis's whereabouts. He was currently residing in an apartment in an expensive part of Chicago.

It wasn't lost on Shane that the last time he'd talked to Wyatt the man thought that Ben was also here in the Windy City. He didn't believe in coincidences.

Quickly hitting the road, Shane and Arden had managed to make it to Chicago before midnight. After getting some much needed rest, they'd go see her uncle tomorrow. She had more than a few questions for the man.

Arden had been quiet most of the drive from Indianapolis to Chicago and Shane had let her be. She needed a chance to deal with everything she'd learned without him pushing her or trying to make things better.

The fact was…things were pretty terrible. Awful. Screwed. She'd been blindsided today and all he could do was be there for her. He knew her well and eventually she would come to him and tell him what she needed. Until then he would stay close and show her how much he loved her.

He tossed their bags on the king-sized bed and then went over to the window to pull the heavy curtains shut. "You can go ahead and use the bathroom if you want. I need to make a few calls."

Instead of heading into the bathroom, Arden sat down on the bed, her fingers fiddling with the bedspread. Shane wished he could fix the blank expression on her face. Her rug of security had been pulled out from under her and it would take time to get her footing again.

"Does Jason know?"

"He doesn't need to know. No one does. This is your secret to tell, not mine."

Her lips turned up at the corners. "I'm stuck between being glad I'm finally finding out the truth about my life and horrified, wishing that I was still living in ignorant bliss. I wonder how my dad – I mean, Ben – was able to keep this a secret for so long. I never would have guessed in a million years."

Sitting down next to her, he lifted her up and placed her back down on his lap, his arms holding her close. Rubbing up and down her spine, he tried his best to sooth her ravaged emotions. "Let's face it, honey—Ben played most of life close to his vest, both personal and business. We only saw what he wanted us to see, but I will say this because I believe it. Ben Cavendish loves you. I can see it when he looks at you or talks about you. There's more to being a father than biology."

Resting her head on his shoulder, he heard her sigh heavily, her breath warm on his neck.

"I know and I think you're right. But his love has been the

obsessive kind. He's always wanted to control my life as much as I would allow it."

"I know that all too well," Shane agreed. "I think that has more to do with Ben's personality than him not being your true father. I bet he would have been like that either way."

Her entire body was shaking and he tightened his hold on her, rocking her back and forth, waiting for the tears that didn't come. It was as if she was cried out or completely numb and it worried the hell out of Shane. When she did start feeling again it wasn't going to be a pretty thing.

"I'm scared."

He pushed back a stray strand of hair behind her ear, rubbing the silky tresses between his thumb and finger. "What are you scared of? What can I do to make it better?"

"I'm scared of what else I don't know. What lies around the corner and is it going to jump out at me like one of those creepy jack-in-the-boxes when I was a kid? I think I've had just about as many surprises as I can take."

Shane didn't see that she was going to get a reprieve. Even if David Hollis didn't have any bombshells to share, when the killer was finally unmasked that would surely be a shock to her heart even if she already suspected her father.

"You're a strong woman and I know you'll be able to survive this. If I haven't told you, I'm so proud of how you've dealt with everything so far. You amaze me." He pressed soft baby kisses to the top of her head. "I love you, just remember that. You're not alone anymore."

If Shane had his way, she'd never be alone again.

"I love you too and I'm so grateful you're here." She lifted her head and brushed her lips against his, caressing his unshaven jaw with her fingertips. "Do you think he did it?"

He'd thought about little else on the drive to Chicago. He had no doubt that Ben was capable of killing if he needed to, but had he lashed out at someone he loved, taking his daughter's mother? That was extreme even for Cavendish. He'd doted on Arden, but then perhaps it had been out of guilt.

"I don't know. He had motive but that doesn't mean he did it. They can't prove that he came back early from his business trip. It's just Destin's theory because, frankly, he doesn't have any proof pointing any other direction. We need to talk to your uncle and your father. Conveniently, I think they're both here in the city."

"Are you going to call Wyatt?"

Shane stood, lifting Arden and setting her on her feet. He gave her a light smack on the bottom and pushed her toward the bathroom. "Just as soon as you get in that bathtub. Have a good long soak and then I'll pour us some wine from the minibar."

She pulled her pajamas and toothbrush from her suitcase. "After the day I've had, make it a whiskey."

He watched as she disappeared into the bathroom and then came the sound of water filling the tub. Pulling his phone from his pocket, he pressed a few buttons, anxious to find out the latest.

"Wyatt? It's Shane. Have you located Ben? Things have taken a turn and we really need to find him right away."

✦　　✦　　✦

THE POLICE CARS and ambulance out front of David Hollis's

apartment building in the tony Lincoln Park area of Chicago weren't a positive sign. Arden's uncle wasn't the only tenant but with the luck they'd been having, these emergency responders weren't there by mistake.

Arden grabbed onto Shane's hand. "This doesn't look good."

"There are other tenants in the building. It could be for any one of them. It's probably just a coincidence."

Shane almost sounded convincing.

"What floor does he live on again?"

He'd told her once but she was naturally rattled about the entire situation. "The top floor. Apartment 302."

Sidestepping the vehicles parked at the curb, they crossed into the sumptuous building foyer complete with marble floors and chandelier hanging from the tin-tiled ceiling. Shane pressed the button for the elevator and wrapped an arm around Arden's shoulders. She'd managed to get some sleep last night and was looking much better this morning. She'd told him over breakfast that she still felt numb inside and Shane couldn't argue that was probably for the best. There was time later to cry, scream, and generally fall apart.

The elevator dinged and the doors slid open revealing a man on a stretcher, two EMTs, and two other men, one in a cop uniform. One look told him the worst and he heard Arden's gasp of shock as her uncle was rolled toward the ambulance.

Her knees must have given out because she seemed to fall slack against him and he propped her up, even as he reached out to the two men trailing the stretcher.

"Excuse me. Is that David Hollis? What happened?"

The taller man in a suit whirled around with a scowl on his

face, and stepped forward, clearly trying to intimidate. "Who are you?"

Shane didn't back down, holding the man's gaze easily. "I'm Shane Anderson and this is Arden Cavendish. She's Davis Hollis's niece. We came to Chicago to visit him."

The man seemed to relax a little but there was still tension in his jaw. "I'm Detective O'Leary and I'm afraid I can't give any details. If you actually are Mr. Hollis's next of kin you can see him at the hospital. They're taking him to the University of Chicago Medical Center. Now if you will excuse me, I have work to do."

With that the detective strode out of the building leaving Shane and Arden standing there by themselves.

"Should we head to the hospital?" Arden asked, her face pale again as she tried to grapple with the latest blow. Life was being very cruel to the woman he loved and it was his job to get her through this.

"I guess we should. Are you going to be okay, princess?"

She looked up at him, her expression blank, which scared him a little. He'd be watching her closely today. "This numbness is coming in handy. I don't really feel anything, to be honest. It's like my entire body is encased in ice but I can hear myself breathe and every beat of my heart. It's weird and kind of scary. What happens when it goes away?"

Bad things.

"We get a fifth of Jack Daniels and sit on the dock by the lake. Or we go for a ride on the bike for miles and never come back. We do whatever the hell you want for as long as you want. It's all about you right now."

"This isn't fair to you," he heard her murmur under her breath as they exited the building.

"Life isn't fair. Now let's get a taxi and go see your uncle. In the meantime, I'll call Jason and see if he has any connections in the Chicago Police Department. I don't think that detective will be sharing any details of what happened here anytime in the near future."

"Can this get any worse?"

Shane stopped in his tracks and yanked her into his arms, burying his face in her blonde curls. "Do not challenge the universe like that. Are you a glutton for punishment?"

Because things could indeed get worse. Much, much worse.

Chapter Twenty-Three

E VERY HOSPITAL IN the world smelled the same. Alcohol. Disinfectant. And illness.

In her thirty-five short years, Arden had spent way too much time in hospitals. While the care she'd received from doctors and nurses had been nothing short of amazing it didn't mean she enjoyed hanging out in the place where they kept the sick people.

Arden shifted on the uncomfortable sofa in the waiting room. Shane had managed to convince the doctor that she truly was related to David Hollis and consequently they'd promised to update her on his condition. They seemed to be relieved that there was someone that cared about his health.

"You okay?"

"No. No, I'm not okay. I hate hospitals. Too many bad memories and they're starting to eat away at the numbness. I'm not sure I want the luxury of emotions at a time like this. It's easier to feel nothing."

"Easier but not necessarily better. I'm not a huge fan of hospitals either. I spent a week in one less than a year ago."

Whipping her head around at the flash of pain that poked at

her chest, she placed a hand on his muscled thigh to brace herself. "Why were you in the hospital?"

A smile played around his lips. "Got shot."

Her heart stuttered in her chest at his words. "Shot? You were shot? Why? How? What the hell, Shane?"

"Didn't you notice the scar on my stomach?"

Actually she had, but somehow it hadn't registered that it might be anything bad. She'd assumed it had been something routine and non-threatening. Like a hernia.

"I did but it didn't occur to me that you'd been shot. You were shot? Holy crap, how did I not know that?"

"You were in New York. And yes, I was shot in the abdomen in a shootout at a gas station. Some bad guys were trying to kidnap my cousin's girlfriend and take her to her crazy ex-stalker boyfriend. I guess you could say I took one for the team. Anyway, they airlifted my ass to Salt Lake City and I had surgery and was in the hospital there for about a week."

His tone was so casual he might have been describing taking out the garbage.

Raising a hand to her forehead to try and make the room stop spinning, Arden thought she might either faint or throw up. Maybe both.

"A shootout? Shane Anderson, why were you somewhere people were shooting at each other? You're a wealthy business-man. The most dangerous thing you should be doing is three martini lunches."

He patted her hand comfortingly. "I was helping out West. We were trying to protect his girlfriend and things went awry. Trust me when I say that normally my life isn't near that exciting."

"I hope not. We just found each other again. I don't want to lose you."

"I told you before I'm not going anywhere."

A short, graying man in green scrubs came through a set of swinging doors and headed straight for them. "Are you family to David Hollis?"

Arden jumped to her feet. "I'm his niece. Can you tell me if he's going to be all right?"

The doctor rubbed the back of his neck and winced. "Your uncle is in very serious condition. He was shot in the chest and has been taken into surgery. You may want to go home as it could take six to eight hours before you hear anything. We can call you when he's out of recovery and in a regular room."

There was no way she was leaving. "Thank you but I think we'll stay."

"Suit yourself. If you do leave to eat or anything, just give your cell number to the nurse's station so they can get in touch with you."

The doctor turned to leave but Arden still had questions. "Wait, how did this happen?"

"That I don't know. You'll have to ask the police. We weren't given any details."

Shane stood and pulled his phone from his pocket as the doctor disappeared behind the swinging doors. "I'll call Jason and see if he has had any luck finding out some details. If not, maybe we can bribe a journalist or something. That worked last time."

"Last time? When you were helping West?"

"No, when I was helping Travis find a killer. His fiancée was suspected of the crime so we needed to find the real murderer."

Arden stared at Shane, realizing they had been apart for a long time. "What the hell have you been doing the last fifteen years? It's like you're James Bond. Can I expect this behavior in the future? Do I need to buy you a bulletproof vest for Christmas?"

Shane winked and grinned, showing off that dimple in his cheek. "Baby, James Bond has nothing on me. Now what are we going to do for the next eight hours?"

Worry.

✦ ✦ ✦

THEY ATE LUNCH at the restaurant across from the hospital. It was ordinary burgers, fries, and several varieties of chicken sandwiches but by noon Arden had been starved. They could have served all you can eat gruel and she would have scarfed it down gratefully.

"You're doing great, Arden. I'm really proud of you."

As much as she loved this man – and she did love him – the cheerleading was beginning to get on her nerves. He was walking around her as if on eggshells waiting for her to either explode or perhaps simply melt into a puddle. She wasn't a grenade with the pin pulled and she didn't want to be treated like she was.

"Thank you," she said through gritted teeth. "But I wish you wouldn't keep saying that."

His brows pulled together and his smile vanished. "I'm sorry. It bothers you?"

She didn't want to hurt his feelings because he'd put up with all her bullshit on this trip and so many other things she couldn't even begin to list. He had the patience of Job and she'd meant it earlier when she'd said it wasn't fair. He was doing all the giving and she all the taking. She couldn't expect him not to get damn tired of it eventually. Maybe she should be pussyfooting around waiting for *him* to explode.

"It bothers me," she replied, knowing she had to be honest. Not wanting to hurt each other was how they got in trouble last time. "I know we're both waiting for my meltdown but I feel a little like an animal in the zoo. You're observing me hoping that when the shit hits the fan it won't be too bad."

"I'm just worried about you. Are you still feeling numb?"

Taking a moment to answer, Arden thought hard about how she felt at this very moment. She'd been avoiding taking any sort of inventory but that couldn't, and wouldn't, last forever.

"I'm not sure. I don't really know how I feel right now except that it's a mixture of so many emotions. I feel angry at my father and grandmother that they kept so many important things from me. I feel hopeful that my uncle will live through surgery and I'll get to meet and talk to him. Even if he isn't my real father I'd like to get to know him, especially since he loved my mother. And I feel sad that you and I lost so many years. Even though I can't be sorry because I did what I thought was right at the time, it's still sad. We loved each other all along. When I left, I only wanted you to be happy."

That was a bunch of sloppy emotion and so far she'd been able to control it but she didn't know how long that would last.

"I was happy...in a way. I just wasn't happily in love." He grinned and bumped her foot under the table with his own.

"You're worth the wait."

The ice cube encasing her heart cracked a little. "So are you."

His fingers played with hers across the table. "Did you love your husband?"

The flash of hurt in Shane's eyes when he asked the question made the guilt churn in her gut. "I cared about him as a person but we were really friends. We both went into the marriage with eyes wide open and I hoped that we could be happy with friendship and respect. Turns out it wasn't possible. He fell for his assistant and last I heard they were very happy together."

"I can put a hurt on the guy for you, if you want."

She was tempted but Michael was the past. He didn't deserve any more of her thoughts.

"Save the offer for my father. I have a feeling the next time I see him things are going to get ugly."

Shane paid the check and they left the restaurant to head back to the hospital. Standing on the front sidewalk, he helped Arden pull on her jacket, tickling her ear with a strand of hair. He was standing close to her, their bodies touching, so when he froze she felt it instantly. He was staring across the street to the entrance of the hospital.

Her own gaze followed to where a man was climbing out of a cab. "What?"

"That's your dad."

She did a double-take and realized Shane was right. Her father, the man they'd been searching for, was paying his cab fare. She waved her arms in the air and hopped up and down.

"Dad!" she bellowed as loud as she could. She wouldn't let him get away from her after everything they'd gone through when he disappeared. "Ben Cavendish, look over here!"

The yellow taxi pulled away, leaving her father standing on the sidewalk staring right back at them. Shane grabbed her hand and they started to cross the street.

That's when Ben ran.

Chapter Twenty-Four

BEN CAVENDISH DIDN'T have a prayer of being able to outrun Shane. The younger man kept himself in top shape at the gym and with a pickup game of football with a bunch of guys at the park once a week when the weather was decent. Ben, on the other hand, might watch what he ate but he hadn't done anything more than a brisk walk in years. The outcome had been decided far in advance.

Reaching out his hand, Shane grabbed Ben's arm as the older man darted down an alleyway. Slamming him into the brick wall, Shane placed his elbow under his hopefully future father-in-law's chin and got right in his face. He was pissed the hell off that someone who was supposed to love his daughter had been so selfish.

"Stop struggling and tell me where in the fuck you've been," Shane growled. "Arden has been worried sick and damn if you don't have a hell of a lot of explaining to do. She's found out a thing or two about you, Ben, and guess what? None of it's good, not that it shocks me."

Ben's hand came up to push Shane's arm away. "Let me go. I won't run."

Loosening his hold but not stepping back, Shane snorted in derision. "It wouldn't matter. I'd just catch up with you again."

Ben's gaze darted up and down the alley, a sheen of sweat on his forehead. "Where's Arden?"

"I left her at the entrance to the hospital. But I think we should start asking the questions. Are you ready to start telling the truth for once in your completely self-absorbed life?"

Ben shoved Shane but it barely moved him from where he stood. Not long ago, the older man might have been able to mix it up more but now he looked aged and defeated. Even his face looked grayer and with more lines, along with the purple circles under his eyes. Ben looked like he hadn't had a decent night's sleep in days.

Good. Neither had his daughter and it was all Cavendish's fault.

✦   ✦   ✦

THE THREE OF them were back in the restaurant, this time with cups of coffee instead of lunch. Ben kept his gaze on the table, barely able to look Arden in the eye, which angered Shane, but then everything her father did pissed him off in general. A man had to take responsibility for his actions and it didn't appear that Ben was ready to do that.

Shane would have to persuade him.

"I've been worried sick," Arden said flatly, giving her father no wriggle room. "You left with barely a word. I thought something horrible might have happened to you by one of your unsavory business associates. Do you ever think about anyone but yourself?"

"I don't have–" Ben began, but Arden shook her head to stop him from going any farther.

"Save your denials. I've known for a long time. I'm not a little girl anymore." She leaned forward, tears shining in her eyes. Underneath the table, Shane placed his hand on her thigh and squeezed, letting her know he was there. "In fact, it looks like I'm not even your little girl at all. Did you know that? Did Grandmother? Were you ever going to tell me the truth about my mother and David?"

Ben's head jerked up and his eyes grew wide. "What–What do mean? Of course you're my little girl."

"The coroner's report says something different. You and Mom can't both be O when I'm A positive. Is David my real father?"

His face growing red, Ben pounded the table with his fist and heads whipped around to stare. "I am your real father. I raised you. David wasn't capable of taking care of himself, much less a wife and child. I love you, Arden, and you are my daughter, blood or not. I tried to give you the best life I could and part of that was moving you out of Hemingdale and away from the past."

Shane felt the tension leak from Arden's body. "Then he is my biological father."

Ben shrugged, his lips in a grim line. "What does it matter after all this time? He's a fuck-up and always has been. I'm your father in the ways that matter."

"Yet you were coming to the hospital to see him," Shane stated, not feeling even a particle of sympathy for Ben. He'd brought all this on himself. If Arden never spoke to him again, she'd be justified. He'd lied and obfuscated about some pretty damn important things.

"He is my brother." The older man hesitated and then exhaled heavily. "The fact is it might be partially my fault."

Shane didn't know what Ben was talking about, but again the man wasn't willing to accept any responsibility.

"What are you talking about, Dad? What might be your fault?"

"Partially my fault," Cavendish corrected. "It's not all my fault. David was acting crazy, yelling accusations and waving the gun around telling me to leave."

"A gun?" Shane groaned and struggled to rein in his temper. Ben Cavendish needed a good punch to the gut. Hollis might as well. "I think you need to start from the beginning."

Ben took a gulp of his coffee and didn't speak right away, obviously formulating his words. To Shane's shame he couldn't help but wonder if Arden's father was trying to make whatever story he was about to tell shine him in a better light.

Cynicism was an ugly thing. But then Ben had never gone out of his way to show Shane any of his good qualities. Far from it.

"Elaine called me a few weeks ago. She said David had suffered a heart attack a few months before and was now making noises about wanting to tell Arden the truth about him being her father. I guess he thought he didn't want to die without talking to her or something. Anyway, once Elaine indicated that David was serious I knew that I had to find him and talk him out of it."

Arden held up a hand. "Wait. Grandmother knew where your brother was all this time? She knew that he was my father?"

"She didn't know his location but she knew he was your biological father." Ben shook his head. "But she talked to him once or twice a year since he left Hemingdale. She thought it was a good idea to keep in touch with him so we could make sure he would stay away from you."

"Because you didn't want me to know that truth?" Arden replied, bitterness in her tone. "Heaven forbid that I should have any idea about my life. Even my last name isn't real."

"I changed my name legally so it certainly is your last name." Ben slapped the cup down on the table and a splash of coffee sloshed onto the table. "I was trying to protect you from a murderer, Arden. David is my brother but I firmly believe he killed Susannah. He killed your mother, sweetheart."

Chapter Twenty-Five

ONTHS FROM NOW, Arden might look back on all this
emotional drama with her family and laugh, but right
now all she wanted to do was cry. Every time she thought she
knew the truth there would a twist and she'd end up speechless
and hurting.

"David killed Mom? Are you sure?"

She'd barely been able to get the words out but Shane's
strong arm around her shoulders gave her just enough strength
to spit them out.

"I'm sure," her father answered grimly. "He was there that
night, I just know it. I don't care what all those other witnesses
say. He wanted Susannah to leave me for him and she wouldn't.
He was a drunk, for God's sake. When she wouldn't leave, he
shot her in a drunken rage."

Her gaze flickered from her father to Shane who didn't look
impressed, but then they'd never had much of a relationship, let
alone a good one.

"Is that something you can prove or is this just a theory?"
Shane queried. "Because you had a powerful motive as well. A
couple of them actually."

Ben's face went from red to purple, his anger almost palpable in the small booth they were sitting in. "That's a nasty thing to say, Anderson. I loved my wife."

"But she loved your brother," Shane said smoothly, his eyes narrowed to slits. "He'd fathered a child that you had to take responsibility for and raise as your own. Not many men would take kindly to that."

Ben shook his head vigorously. "I loved Arden. I wouldn't take her mother from her."

"But can you prove it?" Shane persisted.

Her father's shoulders slumped and he shook his head. "No, I can't. According to the cops, David was at a bar and then with a woman all night. They say he couldn't have killed her. But there are witnesses that place David running from the scene."

"One witness. But it was dark that night, Ben, and you and your brother look a hell of a lot alike."

"I was out of town," the older man bit out with a growl. "The police were able to confirm that."

Arden had had enough of this pissing contest. She loved Shane and she loved her father – although she didn't like him very much right now – and somehow they were going to need to learn to get along.

"Stop it. Both of you just stop it." Arden signaled to the waitress for more coffee although she'd rather have a whiskey. "Dad, please continue your story. You went to find your brother, leaving a cryptic note. Was it you that ran me off the road the night of the party?"

Nodding, Ben took another drink of his coffee. "It was Barnes, your grandmother's chauffeur. I told him I was in a hurry to catch a plane. I'm sorry we scared you but I knew if we stopped you'd try and talk me out of leaving or worse, I'd break down and tell you where I was going. I couldn't let you do that."

"So you left your daughter on the side of a dark, deserted road. Great parenting. Did you come straight here?" Shane asked.

Ben steepled his fingers and nodded. "It took a while to find him but I ended up in Chicago a few days ago. When I finally got an address, I went to see him this morning. I went there to ask him to leave you alone but he was yelling that he'd made a mistake letting a murderer raise his daughter. He said he was sober now and that he wanted to get to know you. Hell, I knew I couldn't let that happen."

Ben Cavendish, businessman extraordinaire, once again trying to control her life. That habit needed to be broken. Now.

"That wasn't your call to make," Arden said, putting as much acid into her tone as possible. "I make the decisions in my life. Not you. You and I have a very serious issue with our relationship. If you don't want to be cut completely out of my life you're going to need to learn to respect the boundaries I set."

Ben turned to Shane, anger blazing, almost standing up in the booth. "This is your fault. You've turned her against me. I suppose you told her you still love her or some bullshit like that? Did you tell her you've been fucking your way through the female population of southern Montana?"

"Sit down," Arden hissed, grabbing at her father's arm and tugging until he fell back onto the vinyl seat. "You're not going to do this again. You're not going to play us off one another to get your own way. Shane and I are together again. If you can't deal with that and be happy for us, you know where the door is."

Her previously purple father turned ash gray. "Together? You're...together again?"

Shane grinned and raised his coffee cup as if in salute. "We are, and there won't be any tampering with the relationship this time. Your daughter just might end up an Anderson."

They'd never talked about marriage but they had spoken about commitment and forever. It was still a shock, however, to think that she might become *Arden Anderson* if they didn't screw things up this time.

Ben Cavendish looked like he might have a stroke. "An Anderson? My little girl is not going to become an Anderson. Over my dead body."

Shane shrugged, his smile still wide. "Whatever works."

"Now you stop it." Arden smacked Shane on the arm. "Stop arguing like children. You both are going to have to find a way to get along so you might as well start now."

"I can get along with anyone," Shane declared, casually sipping his coffee. "Just keep Daddy from trying to interfere in our lives and all will be well."

"You foul-mouthed—" Ben snarled but Arden held up both hands before smacking them down on the table, effectively shutting him up. Shit, if she'd known that would work she would have done it years ago.

"Father, please continue your story. Shane, please stop baiting my father."

Shane placed his arm across her shoulders and settled back into the booth. Her father, on the other hand, didn't appear nearly as relaxed as he added sugar to his coffee and then twisting the empty paper packet between his fingers until it was confetti.

"David was waving around a gun and yelling so I tried to get it from him. I was afraid it would go off accidentally. We struggled and the gun went off, shooting him in the chest. I panicked and ran out of the back of the building and went back to my hotel to change clothes. Then I came over here to check on him."

"Did you call 911?" Shane demanded. "Did you put pressure on the gunshot wound until emergency services arrived?"

Ben's gaze had dropped to the table and he shook his head. "No, I said that I panicked. People might think I have motive to want him dead."

Shane snorted and began to laugh but it didn't sound happy. "You do have motive. More than one. So let me understand your story here… You struggled with your brother but you didn't want him dead. But when the gun accidentally went off, you didn't help him in any way, shape, or form, instead leaving him to die in a pool of his own blood and not even calling 911. That literally would have been the least you could do. That's cold, old man, even for you."

Arden wanted to chastise Shane for speaking to her father that way but she couldn't argue with what he said, only the tone he'd used to say it. It did sound horrible and cruel, and a few other things she didn't even want to put names to.

Dammit, it sounded suspicious. She'd already had her doubts about her father's innocence and now his brother – and her father – was fighting for his life on an operating table. Shane had said that he didn't believe in coincidences and frankly neither did she.

She did believe that David had made statements about coming to see her, especially if he'd felt the weight of his mortality after his heart attack. She also believed her father took off secretly to convince him to stay away. Ben Cavendish took secrecy to a whole different level than regular folks.

But everything else? She wasn't so sure. He'd lied to her too many times to give him the benefit of the doubt. And that hurt…thinking her father might be capable of murdering her own mother.

That happy numbness she'd experienced earlier wasn't doing its job. She was angry and in physical pain, and that fury was focused on the older man sitting across from her. Because of the decisions he'd made she was hurting, deeply, and she didn't know when it would stop.

Arden made her decision right then and there.

"Father, listen to me. Shane and I are going to get up and walk over to the hospital to see how David is doing. You can go with us if you like but you may not speak to me or spend time with me unless you go to the police and explain what happened. That will go a long way toward helping me believe what you said."

Ben reared back, shaking his head in denial. "They'll throw me in jail. I can't go to the police."

Picking up her purse, she pulled the strap onto her shoulder. "Then I'm walking out of here. I don't want to hear from you or see you. If you can't be honest and straight then I have to doubt your word. You've lied so many times to me. Both you and Grandmother. You've broken my trust and I can't be around you right now."

Shane seemed to get the hint and slid out of the booth, offering her a hand to help her stand on shaky knees. She'd never stood up to her father in this forceful way before. Yes, she'd told him off many times but this was different. She was prepared to walk away for good if necessary. Cut ties and never look back. Thank the good Lord she had Shane at her side to help her through this.

They were halfway to the door when she heard footsteps behind her and a hand reach out to capture her arm. She turned to see her father, tears welling in his eyes. He looked old and broken, not like the strong man she'd known all her life, but she couldn't let pity weaken her resolve.

"Okay, I'll go talk to them. I'll tell them what happened. I love you, Arden. I'd do anything for you."

Even keep devastating secrets from her.

How many were still out there to discover?

Chapter Twenty-Six

"DO YOU WANT me to order some room service?" Shane called from the bedroom of their hotel room.

They'd gone back to the hospital earlier and been given the news that the surgery had been successful but that David might not wake up for twenty-four hours or more. Due to the severity of his injuries, the doctors were keeping him sedated until his condition improved.

The police had taken a wait and see approach to her father's statement, telling Ben not to leave town. The forensics in the case had yet to come back and of course, David wasn't able to make a statement, so until then it was simply a case of self-defense.

"I'm not too hungry but I know I should eat," Arden called out from her more than comfortable spot in the oversized hotel bathtub with the jacuzzi jets. Shane had insisted she take a soak and try to relax after all the crap she'd been through today.

She hadn't argued.

"What do you want? They have fried chicken, I know you love that."

Her nauseous stomach actually perked up slightly at the

thought of crispy, golden batter fried, artery hardening chicken. She wouldn't eat much of it but if she was going to try and eat she wanted something that tasted good and wasn't healthy at all.

"Sounds good. Also order a gallon of chocolate ice cream and a fifth of tequila."

Shane pokes his head around the door, a grin on his face. "Fried chicken, chocolate ice cream, and tequila? I don't think that's going to help your tummy, baby girl."

Arden pretended to ponder his words. "You're right. Make it vodka."

His laughter was music to her ears. After one of the shittiest days of her life it felt like heaven to retreat from the cruel, cold world and come back here with Shane. He'd been her rock these last few weeks and she could honestly say that she trusted he'd be there no matter what happened to her.

And so much had happened that she hadn't yet processed it all. Her day of reckoning was coming and all the emotion she'd been bottling up was going to rush to the surface; then heaven help them all. She'd seen a therapist during her marriage and it might not be a bad idea to do it again. If any situation called for professional help this was it.

"I ordered dinner and they're running a little behind." Shane rejoined her in the bathroom and began plucking at the buttons on his shirt. "They estimate about forty-five minutes."

His shirt hit the floor.

"I can wait." Arden sat up and folded her hands on the side of the tub where she rested her chin. "May I ask what you are doing?"

Shane grinned and popped the buttons on the fly of his

jeans, the sound echoing off the walls. "Getting naked. I'm going to join you in that bath unless you have an objection."

Did she? After the emotionally draining day she'd had Arden wasn't exactly in an amorous mood. But then every day had been pretty horrible and she wanted to be close to Shane. If she waited for things to be happy and perfect they might never get together.

"Look at me, princess."

His pants flew across the bathroom and hit the door before falling to the floor. His boxers and socks quickly followed.

"I'm looking."

She sure did like what she saw but that glint of mischief was missing from Shane's gaze.

"I'm joining you in the bath but I'm not looking to...you know...start something. I just want to rub your shoulders and tell you everything is going to be okay."

She scooted up in the tub so he could climb in behind her. Relieved and miffed all at the same time, she relaxed back against his chest and let him play with her hair. She wanted him to want her desperately but she loved that he was a gentleman too.

"Is everything going to be okay? Right now it's all shit and every day it seems to get worse. My father is an asshole, my uncle – who really is my father – is in the hospital, my mother was shot by one of them probably, and everyone who said they loved me has lied to me in some way all my life. I'd be furious but I'm not sure who to be mad at first."

Shane's strong fingers kneaded the flesh of her arms, running his palms over the aching muscles of her shoulders. She was tense and cranky and his hands felt like a slice of heaven.

"Let's take this one at a time. Your father has always been an asshole, so no change there."

Arden groaned as Shane found a particularly tight spot at the nape of her neck. "I can see that you two getting along is never going to happen but you're not far wrong. My father has always been a difficult person who kept a lot of secrets, so I guess this isn't any different."

"Then the issue of your uncle. I know this is a shock but it's your decision what you do with this information. You can meet your uncle or not. Get to know him or not. It's up to you. And honestly from what I read in the case files, your uncle wasn't capable of being a decent father with his substance abuse issues. He might be clean now but he wouldn't have been much of a parent. As much as this pains me to say, I think you were better off with Ben."

She trailed her fingertips up and down his muscular thigh, enjoying the feel of skin and the planes of his body. "I hadn't thought of it that way. I've been concentrating more on the feeling that I was deprived but you're right. If David had all those issues then he probably wasn't someone that I wanted in my life. I wonder if he's better now."

"I don't know, but remember that you don't owe him anything. If you decide that knowing him will complicate your life too much then don't let him guilt you into spending time with him. And for damn sure don't let Ben guilt you into not getting to know David if that's what you want to do."

Her father definitely could put the pressure on when he wanted to. He liked to get his way and he wasn't bothered by things like ethics or rules.

"I won't. I do think I'd like to at least meet and talk to him.

Then I'll make the decision if I want to get to know him more. It's weird though to kind of have two fathers."

"Then let's get to number three. We think that perhaps your mother was shot by one of them. It is possible but it isn't for sure."

Arden sat up and twisted around to look at Shane. "Tell me the truth. Do you think Ben did it? Be honest."

He sighed and let his head fall back on the edge of the tub, clearly not wanting to answer. Arden didn't back down, simply waiting him out. She wasn't going to say anything until he did.

"Maybe," he finally conceded with a groan. "I'll admit the evidence doesn't look good but as much as I dislike him, I saw his face in the restaurant today. He seemed pretty sincere that he didn't do it and dammit, I actually believe him. In his own weird, crazy, self-centered way he really does love you and I think that means he wouldn't shoot your mother."

For Shane to say he thought her father was probably innocent was huge. "I'm sure my dad is capable of killing someone but I'm with you on this one. After talking to him today I just don't think he shot my mom. Does that mean David did it?"

Shane shrugged. "He lacks real motive. Ben said that David wanted her to leave your dad for him and she wouldn't so he shot her. But that doesn't make sense to me. Did David love her so much that he didn't want anyone to have her but him? But someone else did have her. And the someone else was also raising his daughter, so he doesn't seem like the obsessive type to me. Past behavior is the best predictor of the future. If he didn't kill your mother when she stayed with Ben after she had you, then what was the trigger that pushed him over the edge that night? I don't see it."

"Maybe she wasn't going to see him anymore," Arden suggested. "Maybe she wanted to make her marriage work."

"Possibly, but that's one of those things that we will never know for sure. David can tell us whatever he wants and we won't be able to confirm it."

Arden laid back down on his chest, Shane's arms wrapped tightly around her in the cooling bathwater. "So if Ben didn't do it and David didn't do it, then who did?"

"It's a long shot but perhaps it was someone else. A random stranger. A robbery gone bad. Or even another person with a grudge that no one knew about. The detective asked the right question...who would benefit from her death? The answer was Ben, of course, because she was cheating on him and she had a trust fund. But did he look deeper? Maybe there's someone else."

Strong hands pushed her to a sitting position and then Shane quickly climbed out of the tub, drops of water spilling down his naked chest and legs.

"What are you doing?"

He grabbed a towel and roughly dried off before throwing it around his lean hips. "I'm going to call Wyatt. I'm going to have him pull your mother and father's finances."

Shane had that intense expression again; not happy, not sad, just focused. "You're kind of scaring me a little. What are you thinking?"

He paused at the doorway, shaking his head. "I'm not thinking anything specific. I'm just doing what West always says to do when you get stuck. I'm going back to basics, and what are the basic motivations for murder? Greed, love, revenge. We know your father's finances are a mess now so maybe they were then too. Maybe your mother wasn't the target that night."

Realization of what Shane was trying to say jolted her heart. Had Ben been the intended victim that night so long ago and her mother simply in the wrong place at the wrong time?

She'd wondered for years when her father's shady business deals might catch up to him. Perhaps they already had...with deadly consequences.

Chapter Twenty-Seven

ARDEN HADN'T EATEN the gallon of ice cream nor drank a fifth of vodka. Getting hammered sounded like a good idea but she knew from experience she'd be sorry in the morning. Consequently she had two perfectly respectable glasses of white wine with her chicken and mashed potatoes. The bath and the comfort food was just what she needed to make herself feel better, and now she and Shane were snuggled up on the bed watching a movie on television to try and unwind from the day.

Sprawled out with her head on his chest, her attention wandered from Reese Witherspoon's legal antics and to everything that had happened since her father had left Tremont.

"Honey...don't."

She looked up to see the man she loved gazing at her with concern. His brows were pulled down and his forehead was wrinkled so she reached up with her fingers and smoothed the lines. Not that they marred his handsome face. He was gorgeous no matter what.

"I can't concentrate on the movie," she sighed. "My mind is going a thousand miles an hour. You'd think I would be exhausted but I'm not sure I'll be able to sleep."

His fingers raked through her hair, massaging the scalp and making her purr like a kitten.

"I can run down to the drugstore on the corner and get you something to help you sleep."

"I don't like taking things but I appreciate the offer. You're pretty nice to have around."

His eyebrow quirked up and that smile hovered around his well-shaped lips. "I am, huh? It's nice to be around, actually. Maybe you should take advantage of having me here."

"Um, in what way?"

He'd assured her he wasn't pressing for sex earlier but when they'd been together before he'd had a high sex drive. From what she'd heard about his love life, that hadn't changed.

"You could ask me to give you a back rub." He raised his hands in a sign of surrender. "Only a back rub. It might relax you enough so you could sleep."

No woman would say no to that offer.

Arden pulled off the t-shirt she'd stolen from Shane and plopped belly first on the mattress. Looking over her shoulder, she gave him a smile. "There's some lotion on the counter in the bathroom."

Chuckling, Shane pushed himself off the bed. "I guess that's a resounding yes. I'll get that lotion, don't move."

She wasn't going anywhere. She was going to lie here and let Shane massage her knotted muscles and feel pampered and loved. Nothing could be better.

He returned and squirted some of the liquid in his hand, the scent of vanilla filling the room. Kneeling on the bed next to her, he rubbed his palms together to warm up the lotion.

"Are you ready?"

She closed her eyes and pillowed her head on her arms. "Absolutely."

His hands – those strong, firm, beautiful, and talented masculine hands proceeded to turn Arden into a quivering mass of jelly, head to toe. He started on her back and shoulders, kneading the tight muscles until she was sighing in contentment before moving on to her bottom, legs, and feet.

Oh, her feet!

His fingers dug into her arches, rubbed the heels and ankles, and even massaged her toes. It was magical and by the time he was done she felt like she was floating on a big, fluffy cloud. She couldn't help but think that if everyone had their feet massaged on a regular basis there would be no wars or crime. People would simply be too darn happy and content.

"I think someone liked her back rub."

Arden buried her face in the bedspread. "Shhhh, no talking. This is a stress free zone. I'm in a bliss state and any little thing could topple that apple cart."

Shane softly chuckled and ran his large hands up her thighs, over her bottom, and then up her spine to rest on her shoulders. "Sounds more like a bossy zone to me. Is there anything else you'd like other than for me to shut up? Some tea, perhaps? Ice cream?"

Lifting her head, Arden peered over her shoulder. "Is there really ice cream or are you pulling my leg?"

His smile was indulgent and he didn't even need to answer. She already knew there wasn't ice cream. "I can order some."

She narrowed her eyes and scrunched up her face. "It's not

nice to tease me in my bliss state."

"Duly noted."

"I really am grateful. I feel a lot better than I did earlier. It's just a lot to take in, you know? I always knew that my family was different but this takes it to a whole new level. A really messed up level."

Shane sucked in a breath and leaned back against the headboard. It didn't take a genius to realize she was about to be on the receiving end of some tough love.

"You have every right to be upset about all of this. You should be angry and feel betrayed. You should stomp your feet and tell off Ben, and then your uncle when he gets better. And don't leave out your grandmother, although at her age you might want to be a little more gentle. The fact is, a lot of people in your life have let you down and you should be pissed."

"But," Arden prompted. "I hear a *but* at the end of that sentence.

"But you can't let this take over your life. Many people have family that let them down, lie to them, and are basically pains in the ass. The sun will come up the next day and you've got to be ready for it. You came back to Tremont to start a new life and honey, we can have that new life. Don't you want to?"

More than anything.

"Everything feels so up in the air." Arden didn't know how to explain the unsettled feeling she'd had since her father disappeared and she found out her mother was murdered. "Nothing is the same."

He leaned forward, criss-crossing his legs. "That's not true. I'm the same and I love you. I want to have a future with you. I think you want that too."

She did. So very much. "I do want that. More than you can know. But I feel like my new life can't start until I bury the ghosts from my old one."

Shane nodded and then tugged on a lock of her hair, giving her that Anderson smile. "Then we better get busy digging some holes because we're going to bury every one of them sons of bitches. This time, honey, no one is getting in the way of our happily ever after."

That's what she was counting on.

"I'll get a couple of shovels."

Chapter Twenty-Eight

THE NEXT MORNING, Shane left a sleeping Arden tucked up in a warm bed while he met Wyatt in the hotel restaurant just off the lobby. The other man was already sitting at a table sipping his coffee while the waitress tried to flirt with him. Clearly from the patient expression on Wyatt Stone's face, the poor girl wasn't getting very far.

"Shane, glad you could make it. Have some coffee."

The waitress poured Shane a cup while he settled into his chair opposite Wyatt. Both of them quickly ordered – Shane the scrambled eggs and bacon, Wyatt the waffles also with a side of bacon – and the waitress bustled away to put in their orders.

"I got your message this morning." Shane dumped some cream in his coffee. "What's going on?"

"First, the ballistics came back on the bullet in Arden's uncle's chest. It matches the gun used in Susannah Hollis's murder."

That was news Shane wasn't expecting. David's motive was weak at best. "Is he awake yet? I would imagine the police would want to talk to him."

"Not yet. But when you see this you won't be concentrating

on him anymore. If I were a betting man – which I am not – I would say that gun was given to him. We'll have to wait until he wakes up to find out by whom because the serial numbers were filed off."

"This case gets stranger by the minute. Do you have anything else for me?"

Wyatt tapped a legal size envelope on the table between them that Shane hadn't noticed before. "You were right. When I went looking it was right there. I thought it might be something you'd want to see right away."

Shane pulled the piece of paper from the envelope and quickly scanned the contents. His fingers curled into fists and he had to concentrate on relaxing his hands.

"It says Susannah's trust fund was to be turned over to her on her twenty-sixth birthday and she died just thirty days shy of that. She never received the money. Are you one hundred percent sure about this? It's a hell of a coincidence, the timing and all."

Wyatt nodded, his own expression somber. "I am."

Scraping his fingers through his still damp hair, Shane shook his head, his mind still trying to come to grips with what he'd read. "This changes everything."

"Can Arden handle this? She has to be reeling from all she's learned in the past few weeks."

Arden was a strong woman but this would put her to the test. Shane felt a pang of remorse for the speech he'd given her last night. This new blow wasn't going to be something she'd come back from easily. It was going to take time and he'd be by her side every step of the way.

"She's tough and we'll all be there helping her." Their food was placed in front of them and the waitress slid the check on the table before heading back to the kitchen. Shane looked down at his plate, his usually strong appetite suddenly gone. "I guess it's back to Tremont, then. That's the only way to know for sure."

Wyatt shook his head. "I hope I'm wrong."

"Are you wrong a lot?" Shane asked hopefully, but he knew the answer and it wasn't in his favor.

"About women and relationships? All the time. About stuff like this? Hardly ever. I'm sorry, man."

No one was sorrier than Shane.

✦   ✦   ✦

ARDEN'S GRANDMOTHER ELAINE Graham lifted the delicate china teacup to her lips and sipped daintily. She was the first person Arden had wanted to see upon her return from Chicago yesterday. Now they were sitting in Elaine's parlor having tea and cookies while Arden answered her grandmother's questions about her trip.

Elaine was dressed in her usual Chanel suit, this one a frosty pink with white buttons. Her hair was perfectly done and her face made up to look at least ten years younger than her actual age. The perfect matriarch to an incredibly dysfunctional family.

"I'm so glad you're back in Tremont, my dear, and you found that heartless father of yours as well. That's good news."

Arden drummed her fingers impatiently on the arm of the chair. Her grandmother was smiling as if everything was lovely and wonderful when clearly it was not.

"That was the only good news I had, Grandmother. Did you hear me earlier when I said that I found out Mother was murdered and that Ben isn't my real father?"

The older woman sighed and sipped at her tea again before reaching for a cookie from the silver tray. "I did, dear. I suppose we should have told you years ago but the time got away from us and you were happy. There didn't seem any reason to upset you with such news. I mean, it doesn't really make any difference, does it? Your mother is still gone and Ben is still your father."

Gasping, Arden almost dropped her teacup at Elaine's matter-of-fact tone.

"Grandmother, Ben isn't still my father. Not really, anyway. And Mother's unsolved murder is heartbreaking. I don't feel like she can rest in peace until I find her killer and see him brought to justice."

"What can you do to solve a murder that happened over thirty years ago? If the police couldn't do it, I doubt you can."

Arden set the cup and saucer on the table between them. "That's why I've hired Jason Anderson's law enforcement consulting firm. With their help, and Shane's too of course, I'm sure they can make some headway. Science has come a long way since then and Shane said that cold cases get solved all the time."

Nibbling at the shortbread cookie, Elaine nodded. "I'm sure they do, dear. And how is Shane? Did you two…kiss and make up, as they say?"

They'd done a hell of a lot more than that but Arden wasn't going to be confessing any of her sins. Not today. She had more pressing matters to deal with.

"We did, but then I think you knew that. Isn't that why you

encouraged me to ask him for help?"

Elaine smiled triumphantly. "You're perfect for each other. Ben should never have interfered. Shane wouldn't care if you could have children or not. He's not that kind of man."

"You're right, he's not. But I'm still very angry with you, Grandmother. You and Father kept so much from me all these years. I understand why when I was a child but when I became an adult you should have said something."

Swallowing down the giant-sized lump in her throat, Arden pressed her palms to edge of the table, the knuckles turning white. Her stomach was turning somersaults in her abdomen and her heart was racing a million miles a minute against her ribs. She had to get herself under control quickly or this was going to go south.

"It was for the best," Elaine sniffed. "I knew it would upset you and I was right. Sometimes the less we know the better."

That was true. Arden would love to go back about twenty-four hours ago but sadly she lacked a functional time machine.

"I can't argue with that logic but I'm still upset. My mother was shot and Ben seems to think David did it."

"And David thinks Ben did it." A smile played on Elaine's lips. A smile that shouldn't be there. She was talking about her own daughter's murder like they were discussing the latest episode of *Sherlock*. "Don't you think one of them did? The police do."

Arden gripped the table more tightly until pain shot up her fingers. "No, I don't think either one of them did it. I don't think you do, either."

Elaine shrugged and picked up another cookie. "I don't remember what I thought at the time. It was many years ago, my dear, and best left in the past. There's nothing to be gained by digging up old hurts and putting them on display."

Funny thing about shovels and digging up ghosts…you're sure to get the crap scared out of you.

Unfurling her clamped fingers, Arden placed them on the arms of the chair. It was now or never. She was losing her nerve and she'd told Shane she could do this. She'd wanted to do this for her mother. It was all she could do for Susannah Hollis. Arden gathered her courage and took a deep breath to calm her destroyed nerves.

"How did you get in and out of the house that night without anyone seeing you? Or did David see you?"

Elaine blinked a few times at the question but then took another bite of cookie. "I'm sure I don't know what you mean, dear. What night? And what about David?"

Arden licked her dry lips and tried again. "The night you shot my mother. Was David there? Did he see you? How did you convince him not to tell the police?"

"I don't understand what you're talking about, Arden. Have some more tea, perhaps that will clear your mind."

For the first time in a very long time, Arden's mind was clear.

And her heart was broken.

"Was the only reason the money? Or were there other reasons you shot her?"

Placing the cookie back on the china plate, Elaine dabbed at the corners of her mouth with a snowy white linen napkin.

"You and Shane were quite busy, but not in the way I

thought. When I told you to ask him for help I assumed you two would fall into bed with one another and forget all about this. I see I miscalculated that one."

A chink in the older woman's armor. A small one, but it was a start.

"I doubt that happens often, Grandmother," Arden offered, holding her breath in a wait and see. "I'm sure you're very detail-oriented."

"I've had to be. There's no excuse for sloppiness in any endeavor. If you're going to do something you owe it to yourself to do it well."

"You must have thought of everything. After all, thirty plus years and not one person suspected you."

"My dear, most people are not very bright. The vast majority of the population is simply waiting for someone to tell them what to do. So I did."

Her grandmother's sense of privilege was breathtaking and it almost left Arden speechless.

Almost.

"You mean the *little people?*"

Elaine sat back on the sofa, a small smile on her lips. "I mean all people."

"And that's why you were never a suspect?"

"I was never a suspect because I never did anything that could be construed as suspicious."

Arden wouldn't win these verbal spars.

"So you're are denying that you shot my mother."

Elaine leaned forward, the blue eyes so like Arden's own as cold as ice chips. "Are you accusing me of killing my own daughter?"

Everything in that moment was amplified. The ticking of the grandfather clock in the corner. The bergamot aroma of the Earl Grey tea and the vanilla in the shortbread cookies. The slight creaking sound as a gust of wind blew the old oak tree outside the window.

"I'm not asking you, Grandmother. I'm stating a fact. You killed my mother. And you did it all for money."

Chapter Twenty-Nine

S HANE HAD BEEN listening in to Arden and Elaine's conversation from the library located right next to the sitting room where they were having tea. The police hadn't had time to get a warrant and frankly, if he hadn't been West Anderson's cousin, they would have laughed him out of the police station when he came to them with his farfetched theory. Even West had groaned and shaken his head when Shane had shown him the paperwork from Wyatt.

"You better be right about this, because if you're not all hell is going to break loose in Tremont," West had warned.

"I'm positive. Trust me."

West and the head of detectives had now put their asses on the line and here they were listening in on a tense conversation. Shane hadn't wanted to send in Arden but she'd argued that she had the best chance of getting her grandmother to confess. In addition, the older woman was hardly a threat to anyone with her advanced age and crippling arthritis. Reluctantly he'd agreed to stay on the other side of the wall but close enough to intervene if needed.

No recording devices could be used without a warrant as this was a two-party state, and Elaine Graham was not going to agree to be taped while Arden tried to wrangle the truth from her. If the older woman did confess West had already warned Shane that the information could be given to the Hemingdale police but it wouldn't be grounds for an arrest. Not yet.

"I think I've heard enough," Shane whispered to West, who had accompanied him and Brandt Dane, the head of detectives. "I'm going in and see if I can help her."

West nodded and Shane stood quietly, opening the door between the two rooms and slipping through. He must have made a noise because the two women, whose heads were close together as if exchanging a confidence, jerked up to see who or what it was.

"Shane," Elaine exclaimed, a smile on her lined face. "Come have a seat. I haven't seen you in so long. Goodness, you are getting more handsome every day. Would you like some tea, dear? Arden, you should pour your man a cup of tea."

With trembling hands, Arden reached for the teapot but Shane patted her leg and shook his head. "I'm not that thirsty, thank you. It's nice to see you too, Elaine. It's been a long time."

"Too long. I must have you and Arden over for dinner so we can catch up. Any wedding plans yet?"

"I think it's a bit early for that but we'll let you know the minute we have plans," Shane replied smoothly. Arden was looking a little frazzled and he'd hated sending her in here alone. This was her grandmother and the entire situation had to feel surreal. It was time to step in. "We learned some very interesting things on our trip, Elaine."

Elaine Graham had never been a warm woman but right

now she was an iceberg.

"That's what Arden was saying but I think she's become confused, poor child."

Feeling Arden stiffen beside him, he placed an arm around her waist, letting his hand rest on her hip. "How about we talk about your husband Charles? He was a very successful businessman from what I could tell. He inherited a fortune and then made another one from his inventions and patents."

The only tell-tale sign Elaine displayed when Shane mentioned Charles was the tightening of her fingers on the delicate handle of the china cup. "My darling Charles was always so clever. Just one of his many wonderful qualities."

Unlike Arden, Shane had no love for this woman so he didn't hesitate.

"But you didn't love Charles. In fact, you hated him. You told the funeral director that you had *won* since Charles died first. You two made each other's lives a misery, didn't you?"

"All marriages have their ups and downs."

"But you and Charles never loved each other. Your marriage was a farce, a nightmare and in the end…when you thought you had won…he struck the final blow. He left every dime of his estate to Susannah, bypassing you completely."

The cup clattered in the saucer, and two flags of color appeared in Elaine's pale cheeks.

"He shouldn't have done that."

"So you set things right," Arden whispered, an aching pain in her voice that Shane longed to be able to soothe. "You killed my mother for the money. Right before she would have come into her trust fund."

Carefully, the older woman set her tea on the table between them, her features more composed than before. "You can't prove any of this."

Shan shrugged. "Maybe, maybe not. But I'm going to try."

Her fingers traced the edge of a lace doily. "Let's say that I did shoot Susannah. Not that I did, but let's say that I did. How do you think I did it, Shane? How did I get away with it all these years?"

Shane leaned forward, his elbows propped on the table and his fingers steepled under his chin. "You bought an untraceable weapon. Probably from one of your staff or maybe even at the youth center where you donated money and time. I'm guessing you parked on the other block and walked between the houses. At that time of night, you wouldn't have been seen and since you'd spent time in the neighborhood you knew who had dogs that might bark or who would leave their porch lights on."

"This is fascinating, isn't it, Arden?" Elaine's gaze touched on her granddaughter briefly but rather coldly before returning to Shane. "Do continue. I love a good fairy tale. I hope this has a happy ending."

"You snuck in the house. I imagine the doors were unlocked as it was a good neighborhood in a small town. You crept up the stairs to the bedroom and waited until Susannah exited the bathroom. She wasn't afraid, of course—you were her mother, so she didn't run or scream. Maybe she even smiled and greeted you, although she would have probably asked why you were there."

Arden turned to Shane, playing along as they'd discussed with West and the detective. "If Grandmother did it, then how did Delilah see David running from the house?"

Shane nodded. "That's a great question and one that's been bugging me. But then I remembered Delilah's statement to us. She said that she was watching 'Dallas' the night of the murder." He straightened in his chair. "I didn't catch it at the time but when I looked at the date of the shooting on the calendar I realized your mother was shot on a Monday night. She couldn't have been watching 'Dallas'. The police didn't take her statement until a few days later and by then Elaine had paid a visit. She convinced Delilah that she'd seen David that night."

Playing with the double strand of pearls around her neck, Elaine smiled. "I had no idea I was so powerful. I can make people see things that weren't there. If only I'd known earlier it might have come in handy."

"You were the single richest woman in the county, so you were quite powerful. Delilah, like so many in Hemingdale, courted your favor. When you were sure that David did it, she was sure as well. Over the years, it became stronger."

"So she shot my mother and escaped in between the houses," Arden replied, tapping her fingers on the table. "But how did David get the gun? Are you sure he didn't kill my mother?"

Shane placed his own hand over hers. "I'm sure. Elaine gave David that gun right after the murder when she gave him money to disappear. She told him that he'd be the biggest suspect, especially with his history of booze, drugs, and women. She gave him the gun and a chunk of money to disappear, which he did quite well until recently. In fact, until this morning David was convinced Ben had killed his wife."

Arden frowned and shook her head. "Father thinks David

did it."

Shane pulled a piece of paper from his pocket and laid it on the table. "Isn't that interesting? I'm betting that Elaine made sure they suspected each other all these years so that no one suspected her. She's been playing them since the beginning using her money as bait. She even gave your father the seed money to start his business here in Tremont. Smart, huh?"

Elaine waved her hand as if everything he'd said was nothing at all. "All this is very interesting but you have no proof. None at all."

Shane pushed the folder paper across the table. "I have proof of the money you gave David just days after the murder. He disappeared not long after that. I also have proof of the cash you've funneled to him over the years along with money you gave Ben."

Her shoulders lifted carelessly. "It means nothing. I'm generous, that's not a crime."

"I also have the trust documents that gave the money to Susannah when your darling Charles died. They were drawn up when she was quite young, so instead of the trust passing to Arden or Ben when Susannah died, it went back to your hands if anything happened to her before she reached twenty-six. In fact, she was killed just a month shy of her birthday so the trust reverted back to you. That's quite a coincidence that the police never picked up on. Unless Susannah stayed alive, Ben was never going to get his hands on that money. Charles and his attorney should have done a better job there, but then he probably never thought you were capable of killing your own child in cold blood."

Unfolding the paper, Elaine scanned its contents before tossing it back on the table. "This is all just an amusing story. You can't prove anything."

Shane rubbed his chin in thought. "David woke up this morning and is being questioned. I'm guessing he's going to tell the police where he got that gun."

"He can't prove it." Her chin lifted as she played with the large diamond ring on her hand. "You can't prove any of this and frankly, I'm tired of this game. None of this matters now. It was a long time ago."

"It matters to me." Arden's words came out more like a croak. "It matters very much to me. Did you kill my mother? Did you?"

She'd stood up and leaned across the table, shaking a finger in the old woman's face. Elaine shrunk back; for the first time her composure slipped, and her lips trembled with…fear? Certainly not of what she'd done or of Arden, but perhaps of possibly going to jail.

"Whatever I've done, I've done for the good of the family."

"I'll take that as a confession," Arden answered shakily. "You know what's even worse about all this? I loved you. I trusted you. But now when I look at you all I see is a monster. A monster that shot my mother and lied to all of us for over thirty years. How do you sleep at night, Grandmother? Does your daughter ever haunt your dreams?"

Elaine's hands were wrung together, the fingers almost white. "I do love you, Arden. When I'm gone all this will be yours."

"Blood money," Arden spat, a few tears making their way down her cheeks. "I don't want what you stole from my mother.

Tell me, was it worth it?"

Something passed over the old woman's face. Shane wasn't sure what it was but it looked positively malevolent. There was no remorse, only arrogance. Elaine Graham was sure she'd gotten away with it, even now when they were confronting her with facts.

"Your mother was a stupid child who didn't have a clue how the world worked. She was ready to leave Ben and throw her life away on that drunken loser David Hollis. With his gambling problem he would have run through my money like water and she wouldn't have stopped him. All I did was make sure that didn't happen."

Arden's nails dug into the back of Shane's hand but he didn't pull away or wince. The mere fact she was holding herself this together was a miracle and a testament to her strength.

"Just one problem," Shane responded, struggling to keep his own emotions in check. The instinct to protect and comfort his woman almost derailing this entire conversation. "The money didn't belong to you. It belonged to Susannah. Or it would have in a matter of weeks."

He pulled Arden's trembling body closer, protectively wrapping both arms around her torso. Her eyes had turned from their normal soft blue to a stormy gray, betraying the tumultuous feelings that he was sure were careening inside. None of this was fair. She'd done nothing to deserve life slapping her across the face like this and he'd been helpless to stop it or protect her.

"I've grown bored with this topic." Elaine lifted the china cup and took a sip. "You won't be able to prove any of this. What you have is circumstantial and my lawyer will have any so-called evidence you think you may how thrown out before it ever gets to trial. You of all people should know, Shane Anderson. There are two judicial systems in this country. One for the rich and one for everyone else. I'll never see the inside of a court-room, let alone a jail cell."

West and Brandt took that moment to saunter in and Elaine's eyebrows flew up in surprise, betraying for only a moment a glimpse of vulnerability. She was afraid of jail, whether she admitted it or not. It was probably the first time since her "darling Charles" passed away that anyone had called her on her bullshit.

Shane stood, helping Arden to her feet. She squeezed his hand and lifted her chin as if ready for battle before turning back to her grandmother.

"You may never see a trial or a jail cell, but I promise you this. I will make sure everyone in Tremont and Hemingdale know everything that we now know. They can draw their own conclusions but at the very least they'll be suspicious. Your once spotless reputation as a kindly matriarch will be ruined and people will recognize you for what you are. A sociopathic killer who shot her own daughter for money. I will not rest until you are ostracized from society and the only friends you have are the staff you have to pay to work here. Take a good look, Grand-mother, because you'll never see me again."

With that, Arden whirled around and marched out of the parlor, her head held high. Shane's chest swelled with pride as she made her exit. She had a spine made of solid steel and had stood up to what would have crushed a lesser woman.

West smiled at Elaine but it didn't reach his eyes. "I'll be talking to the other members of the town advisory board about holding a special meeting regarding your membership. There's a morals clause in the bylaws and we have the ability to hold special investigations into the background and activities of our board. I'm guessing you wouldn't want us to do that."

Brandt crossed his arms over his chest and nodded. "I'm also handing this information over to the Hemingdale police, but I think I might do some investigating here as well. It appears that Elaine has been involved in some of Ben's less than legal business dealings by providing the money. I bet the SEC might be interested in some of her trading activity as well. Having the Feds poking into her life should keep her and her attorneys busy for the next ten years or so."

Shane leaned forward so his palms were flat on the table and he could look into the older woman's eyes. "I'll be around. I won't give up. I'll be pushing this with every law enforcement official that will talk to me until the day you take your last breath. I'll get justice for Susannah...and Arden. You stole her mother away from her, and for that you will be held accountable either by a court of law or by the court of public opinion."

Turning on his heel he also walked out, anxious to get to Arden. She'd confronted the worst and now it was time for her to heal. He'd be there every step of the way, holding her hand and loving her.

Chapter Thirty

THE NUMBNESS THAT had been so welcome before had speared its icy tendrils into every pore and cell of Arden's body to the point she feared she'd never feel anything ever again. She'd expected to be in excruciating emotional pain, but she felt nothing. Nothing at all.

Shane had brought her back to his home and placed her in front of the fireplace, a glass of whiskey in her hand. She'd said little since they'd left her grandmother...no, Elaine Graham. That woman didn't deserve to be called family or even a human being. She'd callously extinguished her daughter's life and for that she'd lost the right to belong.

Kneeling next to her, Shane stroked her hair and cheek, although in her state she could barely feel his fingers. "You're going to be okay, baby girl. Maybe not today, and maybe not tomorrow, but one day. You'll wake up one morning and suddenly things won't looks so bad and you'll find that you're happy. You'll want to make plans for the future and you won't think about the past so much. I know that seems far away but it will happen, and sooner than you think."

She couldn't picture such a day but she trusted Shane to

speak the truth. The fact was she was more concerned about this moment than some future she couldn't picture. Because right now it felt as if she could go a few rounds with a boxing champion and never feel a scratch, bruise, or broken bone. It was like she'd taken ten times too much cold medicine and she was looking at herself from the outside as a spectator, not participating in her life but simply watching it.

Slamming the glass down on a side table, she turned and clutched at Shane's shirt, the material crumpling in her grip. "Kiss me."

Confusion flickered over his features but he did as she asked, pressing his warm lips to her cold ones and letting his tongue trace her lower lip before giving it a nibble.

She felt nothing.

"Harder. More."

Jerking him closer, their lips met again and she ground her body against his in an effort to create some sensation, whether unpleasant or pleasurable. At this point, she didn't much care which.

She bit down on his tongue and he groaned, pushing her back to the rug, his muscled body covering hers. Her nails dug into his shoulders and she wrapped her jean clad legs around his waist to keep his weight pressing her into the floor.

Shane's lips wandered over her jaw and down her neck, stopping to nip at a spot on her shoulder before soothing it with his tongue. She moaned in delight, welcoming the sensation of pain and then pleasure, her arousal quickly building.

Reaching down, she clawed at the fastening of his jeans, desperate to pull them off and have him inside of her. He sat back on his knees and covered her hands with his own, his expression puzzled and concerned.

"We'll get there. Slow down."

He didn't understand. She tugged again at his shirt, ripping at the buttons until they flew across the room and skittered on the hardwood flooring. His bare and tanned chest called to the baser instincts driving her and she licked a line from his sternum down to his bellybutton, eliciting a groan from somewhere deep inside of him.

"I can't wait." She looked up at him, hoping he could see the need in her eyes. "Don't make me beg and don't tease. I feel so numb and only you can make me feel something. Take me now, fast and hard. I don't want you to be gentle. Please."

Understanding flooded his gaze and he nodded as his fingers insinuated themselves between sweater and skin. The heat from his palm seared her flesh and she welcomed it, pressing herself even closer and reveling in the white hot flames that seemed to lick along her veins, melting the frost that surrounded her heart.

He stripped her shirt and then her jeans before tugging at his own clothing. She didn't wait for him to add her bra and panties to the ever-growing pile of clothes on the floor, pulling them off and tossing the unwanted barriers away. She couldn't wait to be skin to skin with Shane, his hard body as close to her as possible.

Cursing, Shane managed to extricate himself from his socks and Arden didn't waste a second. She flew at him, shoving him onto his back and attacking his nipples with her mouth and tongue, drawing a ragged moan from his lips. His grip tightened on her hips and she wriggled her bottom in approval as she straddled his thighs, his already hard shaft pressing against her wet slit. She rubbed herself against him before reaching down and wrapping her fingers around his length.

"Wait, baby." His hands stayed her movements, his brow wrinkled in thought. Thinking was way overrated at a moment like this. "Don't we…I mean…shouldn't we…play a bit?"

He was hot, hard, and ready, pulsing with every beat of his heart and she was impatient and dying to feel him inside of her. Foreplay? Unneeded and undesired.

"No time," she replied calmly, levering up on her knees before lowering down slowly, his impressive girth stretching her walls almost painfully. In truth, she could have used a little foreplay but she'd wanted this. It wasn't hurting but it was uncomfortable and she whimpered as she took the last inch, completely and totally full. "Need you now."

His grip on her bottom wouldn't allow her to move until his impalement was much more pleasurable. Her desire to move overtook rational thought and she leaned forward, her palms splayed on his rock hard chest. "Hard. Rough. Make me feel it. I want to be thinking about this tomorrow."

For a moment, she thought he might deny her but then he nodded, his fingers sliding up her spine and around her ribcage to cup her breasts, his thumbs rubbing back and forth over the hard tips. "Take what you need. I love you."

"I love you too."

Because he loved her and she loved him she was confident that he would never truly hurt her. His protective instincts were in full swing and she could feel him holding back as she rose up and then slammed back down, letting her swollen clit rub against his groin. It sent a streak of lightning up her spine and down her legs and she did it again and again, throwing her head back and moaning Shane's name until she was hoarse and dangling on the edge of the cliff.

Bracing her hands on his chest, she gyrated her hips in a circle so that he hit every sensitive spot inside of her, raising her arousal into the clouds. His fingers plucked at the pebbled tips of her breasts, giving them a rough pinch every now and then. Her toes curled at the bite of pain with her pleasure and she urged him on wordlessly by arching her back in silent offering.

Sweat trickled down her back and her thighs burned and ached as she rode Shane, desperate to find her release. How this man read her mind she didn't know, but he must have. Reaching between their bodies, he found the sensitive button, pressing and rubbing with his thumb until the tight coil in her belly unwound and pleasure exploded, humming through every atom of her being.

Shane found his own completion, his rough hands tangling in her hair when she collapsed on his chest. He folded her into his arms, stroking her back soothingly and whispering silly, loving words.

As the pleasure ebbed away, she realized they'd been successful. The numbness that had dogged her for days had receded and the pain she'd expected was beginning to grow and expand. Holding onto Shane, she closed her eyes and pressed her head to his chest. He would keep the bogeyman away, at least for now.

But hiding behind Shane wouldn't solve this.

She had to face it head on.

✦   ✦   ✦

"ARE YOU HUNGRY?" Shane asked as they stretched out on the couch to watch some television later that evening. "I think I have some ice cream if you're in the mood for dessert."

Arden shook her head and burrowed farther into his chest. "I'm full. And tired. Maybe I should go home so you can get a good night's sleep. I know you have to go into the office tomorrow. I'm sure they're missing you."

"I was able to keep up with things," Shane shrugged, flipping through the channels until he found the weather. "I am beat and as soon as I see what the weather is going to be then we can hit the sack. Notice I said we. You're not going anywhere. We sleep together now."

The tension in her shoulders would have been imperceptible to anyone but Shane. He knew her too well and this wasn't going to be something he liked.

"I'll spend the night then."

The silence hung heavy around them. So much was unsaid and his frustration grew as she continued to stay quiet.

"You can talk to me."

Her fingers stroked his bicep through the cotton of his shirt and he heard her exhale on a sigh, her breath warm on his skin. "You're going to be angry."

Shane struggled to sit up, dislodging her from her comfortable position so he could look her in the eye. Her gaze was downcast as if the pattern on the sofa cushions was the most fascinating thing she'd ever seen, and Shane crooked a finger and placed it under her chin, lifting her face so she was forced to look at him.

"I might be mad or might not. Why don't you tell me what's

on your mind?"

Pulling her knees up to her chest, she wrapped her arms around her legs, hugging them close, possibly to feel protected or perhaps to shut him out. Neither one was good as he didn't want to think she felt threatened by his closeness nor that she wanted to be alone. "I'm leaving in the morning. I'm going back to Chicago. I want to get to know my father…David. I think it's the right thing to do."

Shane stood, his hands tightening into fists. He couldn't lose his temper or beg her to stay. Neither reaction would make him look sane or convince her not to go. He needed to stay calm and reserved, making his case with logic, not emotion.

"Then I'll have them gas up the jet and go with you. I can work remotely just as I have been."

He knew her answer before she gave it. Her gaze dropped again and her cheeks turned pink. "I think I should go alone."

He'd been pacing back and forth but he came to a halt. "I thought we were done with being alone. I thought we were a team now."

Burying her face in her hands, Arden choked down a sob. "We are a team and I do love you. I want you with me all the time but…"

"But what?"

He didn't care that the words came out terse. His anger was rising and he could feel the heat on the back of his neck.

"I'm a mess." Arden threw her arms in the air, a groan on her lips. "I'm messed the hell up, Shane, and you know it, so don't pretend you don't. My grandmother is a murderer, my father isn't my father, my mother was shot, and my uncle is my biological dad. Come on and cut me some slack here. I need to find a way to deal with all the shit that's been thrown at me these last weeks."

He held up his hands in surrender. He couldn't argue her point but he could argue her method. "You're right. You've been through the wringer and endured more than any human should have had to since Ben disappeared. But you don't have to deal with this all by yourself. I can be there for you."

Her eyes were shiny with tears. "Actually, I do. I need to know that I can stand on my own two feet and kick this in the balls. This is my emotional journey, Shane, not yours. This is my battle to fight and win. I love that you want to help me but this isn't your war. If I can't do this on my own then I'm no good for us. I need to come to you strong and independent, not needy and weak. I want you to know without a shadow of a doubt that I'm with you because I want to be. Not because I *need* to be."

Shane wanted to yell. Scream. Beg. Reason. Anything that would get her to stay or a least allow him to go with her, but that determined little chin was lifted even as a tear slid down her cheek.

Well, shit.

"I don't want this," he finally said, not able to hold the truth back. "I hurt when I'm not with you. We spent fifteen years apart and it felt like a part of my heart and soul were missing. I don't want to feel that way again."

"I don't either," she said softly, standing and pulling him into her embrace. Her ear rested on his chest and he was sure she could hear the heavy thud of his heart. He wasn't as sure it would keep beating if she left. "I felt the same way, missing you every single day. I don't want to leave you but circumstances have dictated something we didn't plan. I will seek a professional to talk to but I think I need some time to just…be. I need some space to wrap my head around this and make sense of the new reality of my life. I still love you and that won't change."

He rubbed his chin on the top of her head, her curls silky against his skin. "I don't want to lose you again."

She pulled back and brought up her hands to cup his face. "Never. That's never going to happen. We can talk every day on the phone, or Skype, or text. I'll be available to you twenty-four hours a day. I'm yours and you're mine. I'm just going off for a little while to get my head together."

"How long?"

He was terrified of her response.

She gave him a watery smile. "I don't know. If I had that answer I probably wouldn't need to go at all. But I do know one thing that's absolutely, unequivocally true." She lifted his hands to her lips and pressed kisses on his rough knuckles. "My love for you is so strong there's no way I could stay away for a long time because every day apart from you will be sheer torture."

Then don't go. Stay with me.

"If you need anything—"

"I'll call you right away," she cut him off, already knowing where he was going. "You'll be the first person I talk to in the morning and the last at night. I promise."

He could argue with her all night long but he wouldn't win, and he didn't want to waste the little time they had together at odds. He'd rather be making love.

"Don't stop loving me," he said instead. "Don't forget that

we have a future to live."

More tears spilled from her eyes and slid down her beautiful face. "I'm counting on that. I know this sounds stupid but I couldn't have come this far without your love, and I couldn't go off and do the work that needs to be done if I was alone. Don't stop loving me either."

"I guess if I've waited this long, I can wait a little longer. I just want to lodge my formal complaint about this. We were supposed to ride off into the sunset and live happily ever after."

It was one more hurdle and Shane was damn tired of jumping. When did he get to relax and be happy?

Chapter Thirty-One

S HANE GROWLED AND scowled at the stack of file folders on his desk. He hated paperwork more than he hated spinach or Brussel sprouts. He helped run a multi-million dollar diversi-fied portfolio of holdings including a ranch, oil, and mining, but for some reason he was still stuck with a pile of papers on his desk.

Wyatt Stone stuck his head into the office. "Is it safe to come in? I thought I heard a bear or maybe a puma."

Snorting at the man's feeble attempt at humor, Shane waved him in. Wyatt settled in the chair opposite and stretched out his long legs. For the last few weeks, he'd been digging into Elaine Graham's business dealings so they could turn any findings over to the federal investigators.

"Very funny. You're a laugh a minute." Shane stood and walked over to the small refrigerator located in the corner of the office and pulled out two bottles of beer. It was well after quitting time and the only other people about were the cleaning crew. "When did you get back into town?"

Wyatt checked his watch. "About an hour ago. I haven't even been to the apartment yet but I wanted to come by and give this to you. I'm heading to the farm in the morning."

Stone had a small farm in the middle of nowhere that had been in his family for generations. From what West had said, Wyatt had retreated there after the Army but had been lured out with the promise of work a little more exciting than feeding chickens. But he still liked to go back and spend large swaths of time there away from the hustle and bustle of…people.

Stone was a loner.

Not the crazy, psychotic variety of loner but the kind that didn't have much patience for the stupidity of the human race. Wyatt laughingly said that the older he got the less tolerance he had for people who were hateful or close-minded.

Retrieving a file from his messenger bag, Wyatt traded it for the beer.

"Anything good?" Shane asked, perching on the edge of the desk and taking a drink from the icy bottle.

"It's a mixed bag. I'd recommend a forensic accountant to really dig in and follow the money trail. I think she was the bank behind most of Cavendish's business schemes, both legal and illegal." Wyatt leaned forward, his brow knitted in concern. "You do realize that if we find dirt on your girlfriend's grandmother we're probably going to find it on her daddy too. They could both end up going to jail. Are you sure you want us to keep digging?"

Shane had asked that very question to Arden, but she wrinkled her nose and crossed her arms over her chest with a harrumph as if the very query disgusted her. She'd assured him in no uncertain terms that she wanted to continue. Let the chips fall where they may.

"She and I are both certain this is the right thing to do. She wants the truth known and is well aware it's going to get ugly. Well…uglier than it already is."

"Murder ain't pretty. Is she hanging in there okay? Are you?"

That was the problem. Shane didn't know how Arden was doing. Not really. He talked to her several times a day and they even Skyped, but unless he was there with her, he couldn't truly know if she was getting along well. He missed her and he needed her but she'd asked for this time and dammit, he was determined to give it to her.

Even though it was stupid. They should be working through this together. She wasn't alone anymore and she didn't have to do this all alone like she had the last time she'd left. This time she knew he loved her more than his own life. That had to count for something.

"She seems to be doing well, and spending time with David and Lydia really seems to help. She's growing closer with them and that's a good thing, especially if we send Elaine and Ben to jail."

Wyatt's lips tightened and he heaved a long sigh. "I'll be honest with you. I'm a little torn about sending an almost eighty-year-old woman to jail. I know she's a murderer but she kind of reminds me of my grandma."

Shane wasn't happy about the turn of events either. He vacillated between feeling really shitty and feeling justified. It depended on his mood and the time of day.

"I don't feel great about it myself but she wasn't eighty when she shot Arden's mother. Hell, she's probably right anyway. Her lawyer is already filing motion after motion and trying to block the investigation. She'll die in the comfort of her own home. Her real punishment will be losing Arden. I know that bothers her whether she lets on or not."

"It's not much to pay for taking a human life," Wyatt observed. "Seems like there's no good answer here. Someone will always think we were too tough or not tough enough. Can't win for losing."

Wyatt levered to his feet and set the half empty bottle on the desk. "I should be going. If you need me for anything I'll be at the farm. Where will you be?"

Shaking his head, Shane didn't understand the question. "Here—where would I be?"

"With that pretty girl, of course. According to your brothers and cousins, you're about as useless as tits on a bull these days. Might as well go get that girl and let her know you love her."

Shane had been fighting that urge for weeks. "She asked for time to deal with it herself."

Chuckling, Wyatt picked up his leather messenger bag from its spot next to the chair.

"And you have. How's that working out for you?"

"Fuck," Shane said before he could stop the word from popping out. "Fuck, I'm miserable."

"Are you going to sit on your ass or are you going to do something about it? I haven't known you long, Shane, but the one thing I've noticed about you – all the Andersons, really – is that they don't sit around and complain about their life. They go out and do something about it. Until now, that is."

Shane didn't like the picture of himself as a bellyacher, bitching and moaning about how unfair things were and sitting around with his thumb up his ass. Stone was right. That was not how he lived his life.

Grinning, Shane reached for his cell phone. "Looks like I have a few calls to make."

The first one would be to David and the second to Travis to let him know Shane was taking the jet to Indianapolis. He had a future and he'd put it off long enough.

She might hate him but he couldn't wait any longer.

Chapter Thirty-Two

D AVID HOLLIS HELD up the newspaper. "Do you want part of it, sweetheart?"

Arden was sitting in David's home in Hemingdale having breakfast. After he'd recovered from his gunshot wound, he'd decided he wanted to return to his hometown. Arden had gone with him so they could spend some time together and in addition get to know Aunt Lydia even better.

"No, I'm good." Arden shook her head and dug into her waffles. "What do you have planned for today? I was thinking we could go see a movie or something."

It had become too cold for a walk around the town but she didn't like the idea of David sitting at home either. He was too used to being alone and was having a hard time breaking the habit.

"Lydia mentioned lunch."

David's attention was trained on the sports section but Arden could see the ruddy tone that had taken up residence in his face.

He was smitten with Aunt Lydia and she appeared to be quite taken with David as well. The two were flirting up a storm whenever they were together and Arden couldn't help but hope they might fall in love and get together. After struggling with addiction for so long, he finally had his life under control and it would be wonderful if he could find a woman to share it with.

"You should go then." Arden sipped her orange juice and tried to look nonchalant. "Maybe I'll stay here and call Shane or something."

David's brows shot up and then he laughed, his eyes lighting up with mirth. "My darling Arden, never take up playing poker. You couldn't bluff your way out of a nursery school, but then you get that from me. I lost my shirt at cards and at pool too. Do as I say, not as I do."

She didn't call him dad or father but he'd turned into a loving friend. She was his daughter but she wasn't looking for another parent to replace Ben.

Ben...who was currently not speaking to her because she wanted to get to know David. Her father was acting like a spoiled brat and he'd finally showed how desperate he was to get her home two days ago when he'd told her that she was going to lose Shane if she didn't get back to Tremont. Ben Cavendish had never cared one iota if Shane was in her life or not. He'd simply been trying to manipulate her. Again.

She loved her father but she wasn't going to be his puppet ever again.

"I usually stick to Go Fish," Arden teased, shaking her fork at him playfully. "I just wanted to give you and Lydia a chance to be alone, that's all. You both make a nice couple."

David smiled and shook his head. "You're a sweet girl. You remind me so much of your mother. She'd be so proud of you, honey."

Tears pricked behind Arden's eyes but she welcomed this rush of emotion. Talking with David and Lydia these last three weeks she's learned so much about her mother. It wasn't the same as actually knowing her, but it was closer than she'd ever been and she was damn grateful for this chance.

"I'm not sure why. I'm divorced with no real job. I was a teacher and a pretty decent one but I don't have many accomplishments to call my own."

David folded the paper and set it down on the table. "You found Susie's killer, honey. That's a big accomplishment and one that I am very grateful for. I was a suspect, after all, and I always thought Ben did it. Of course Elaine made sure to drop little hints that she agreed while doing the same with Ben about me. You did the world a service revealing the truth about her. I'm ashamed I let her convince me to run away. She said that I'd be suspect number one and that no one would believe me. Hell, it's probably true. She bought and paid for me but no more. I'm my own man now and I have you to thank for that."

"It was Shane and his family," Arden insisted. "He did the real work. I was along for the ride."

"I think you did more than you're letting on. Speaking of Shane, how is he? Did you talk to him this morning?"

Arden had kept her promise to Shane. He was the first person she spoke to in the morning. She reached for her phone on the bedside table before her eyes were even all the way open, propping herself up on some pillows so they could have a long chat. They usually Skyped each other in the afternoons, and then they had one more phone conversation in the evening before she went to sleep.

She missed him. More than she thought was humanly possible. Knowing he loved her and wanted her home wasn't making this time easy. Spending her days with David and Lydia had helped her make sense of her world but her heart and body ached for the man she'd left behind.

In a way it had been easier when she'd left as a girl. She'd thought Shane wouldn't love her if he found out she couldn't have children. But he truly didn't care and he only wanted her in his life. That was surely the only place she wanted to be. And soon.

But this morning had been different. She'd called him first thing just as she'd done every day since she'd left Tremont, but this time he hadn't answered and the pain had felt like a sword through the heart. He hadn't wanted her to leave in the first place and he might be tired of waiting for her to return.

She thought back to their conversation the night before but it hadn't seemed out of the ordinary.

"I didn't speak with him this morning. I guess he must have had an early meeting. I kept him away from work for quite a while so I know he's been busy catching up."

David patted her hand. "It's wonderful having you here and getting to know you, but I think you're missing your man, Arden. I won't be hurt if you go back to Tremont. Just invite me to the wedding, okay?"

She'd told David her life story, which included her relationship with Shane.

"I don't think that's going to happen anytime soon. I'm not sure Shane's the marrying type after all these years. He's probably pretty used to being on his own."

A skeptical look on his face, David finished the last of his coffee and stood from the table.

"I have some errands to run this morning before we meet your aunt for lunch. It's the Italian place you like so much at noon. I'll get a table for four."

Retrieving his keys from the kitchen counter, he whistled a lilting tune as he headed for the front door.

"Wait. Four? Who is joining us?"

David opened the door but turned and gave her a wink on his way out. "Have a good morning. I won't be coming back here until late afternoon so you have the place to yourself. Lots of privacy."

That was weird. Does he think I'm going to dance around in my underwear like Tom Cruise?

After quickly cleaning up the dishes, she curled up on the couch with her phone and tried to call Shane again. It rang twice but this time he answered.

"Hey, princess. Miss me?"

Her relief was almost palpable and she was sure he could hear her sigh of happiness at the sound of his voice.

"More than you can imagine. I tried calling earlier but I guess you must have been working or out for a run."

"Something like that. I'm sorry I missed your call. Is everything okay there?"

No, I miss you. I wish you were here.

"Everything's fine. I think David and Lydia are smitten with each other. He blushed this morning when I mentioned her name."

She heard his laugh through the phone, rich and warm. "You're playing matchmaker, huh? That might not be a good idea. David has some baggage, sweetheart."

"Everyone does."

"He has more than most but I can see that talking you out of this is a waste of time."

The doorbell rang and Arden craned her neck to try and see out of the front window, but whoever was there was at the wrong angle. "That's the doorbell. Can you hang on for a sec?"

"Sure."

She stood and ran toward the door where the idiot outside was leaning on the bell so it chimed over and over, making the ten feet to the entrance feel like a hundred. By the time she yanked the door open she'd opened her mouth to chew out the offender but one glimpse stopped her in her tracks.

"Cat got your tongue?"

Shane was standing in the doorway with a shit-eating grin and his phone to his ear. He pulled it away and pressed the end button before slipping it into his jacket pocket.

"Shane."

Her voice sounded high and squeaky but he didn't seem bothered by it since he strode in, kicked the door closed behind him, and tugged her into his arms. Their lips crashed together and she was starved for the taste and feel of him. Her hands splayed over his muscular back while his tongue probed for entrance to her mouth. The kiss was hot, sexy, and over much too soon.

Dazed, she allowed him to lead her over to the sofa and pull her onto his lap with his arms wrapped snugly around her.

"Shane," she said again, still not quite believing that he truly was here with her. Perhaps she'd conjured him out of a dream or fantasy.

A dirty fantasy.

"Are you surprised?"

She nodded, not trusting her voice or her brain to put together actual sentences.

"How?" she finally asked, her gaze sweeping him from head to toe. He looked the same. The same smile, the same handsome face, and the same warm embrace that made her feel safer than she ever had in her life. Her heart felt like it would burst with love.

"The usual way." The dimple in his cheek appeared. "An airplane at an ungodly time of the morning so I could get here early and surprise you."

She tilted her head as her uncle's words echoed in her addled mind. "David knew you were coming, didn't he?"

"I might have mentioned it to him. He said you were missing me and I knew I was missing you." Shane's smile fell and his hold on her tightened. "I know you wanted to do this alone and dammit, I really tried to let you but I just couldn't stay away any longer. I love you, Arden, and we need to be together. I can help or I can stay out of the way, but please don't ask me to leave you again. I can't. It's been physically painful to be away from you these last weeks."

Her face flushed and she shifted uncomfortably. "I think maybe you're right. It's been so hard here without you. I've loved getting to know my family but I don't like being away from you either." She leaned forward and pressed a kiss to his lips. "Thank you for coming for me."

"Thank you for not sending me away." Shane looked around the living room. "Where is David?"

A smile spread across her face and she hummed in excitement. It had been too long since she'd been with the love of her life. "He went on some errands. He made sure to tell me before he left that he wouldn't be back until this afternoon and that I'd have privacy this morning."

Shane waggled his eyebrows suggestively. "Privacy? I like the sound of that. What do you suggest we do with it?"

She tugged at his shirt, bringing him closer so she could kiss him again. "I think we should get naked and make some noise. What do you think we should do?"

"Who am I to argue with such a wise decision?" He dipped his head and nipped on her earlobe. "Lead the way."

Chapter Thirty-Three

ARDEN HAD PLANS and every one of them involved both of them without clothes, doing all manner of naughty things to one another. She'd had almost three weeks to ruminate on what she'd do to him the next time she saw him and now here he was in all his naked glory.

And it was glorious.

He'd quickly shucked his clothes while she did the same and then crawled up the length of the bed to where she waited, leaning back against the headboard. He'd reminded her of a panther she'd seen on a nature show stalking his prey. Her body trembled in response and heat shot through her veins straight to her lower abdomen.

His big body covered hers and she loved feeling so small and feminine, but she wanted to show him how much she'd missed him. She wanted to worship him.

"Lie back," she urged, a hand on his shoulder. "Just relax and enjoy."

She felt his chuckle deep in his chest and he settled on his back with his head pillowed in his hands, wearing nothing but a smile. "I most definitely will enjoy. Go on and do your worst."

Her gaze traveled down his body, taking in the part of him that was hard and ready. "Someone is happy to see me."

"Little girl," he growled, low and sexy making her toes curl in anticipation. "Are you going to talk all day?"

That wasn't the plan.

Straddling his thighs, she leaned over and pressed baby kisses to his face, working her way from his forehead all the way to his chin before heading down the long column of his neck. She paused to nip at his Adam's apple and then skipped to his collarbone, ghosting her lips over his sensitive flesh.

He shuddered and moaned as she licked a trail down his torso, stopping off to whirl her tongue around his flat, male nipples, nipping at them with her teeth until his hands came down to grab the back of her head. She giggled at his attempts to lead her farther south but she wouldn't be deterred from her mission, wanting him to know she loved every inch of his body.

Taking her time to lap at his treasure trail, she lazily drew circles with her tongue all the way to his inner thigh, careful not to go near her final destination. She wanted him begging by the time she put her mouth on him.

Because his pleasure was her pleasure, her own arousal had flown into the stratosphere. Honey coated her thighs and her nipples were beaded with excitement. She'd never been with a man that could make her feel this way with barely a touch.

Speaking of touch...

His hands had abandoned the back of her head and his fingers were stroking everywhere he could reach – her shoulders, her arms, and oh yes, her breasts. Shivering with delight, she ran her tongue up the length of his shaft, feeling the velvety skin covering forged steel. She traced the veins as he groaned encouragement and she giggled when his questing fingers tickled under her arms.

"Stop that," she laughed as she tried to twist away but his hold on her was firm. "You're such a goof."

"You're such a tease. Come up here and kiss me properly. It's been too long."

Arden allowed him to lift her up so they were face to face. It only took a second, but she was suddenly flat on her back with one very aroused male on top of her, a feral look in his eyes.

She wasn't the only one with plans, apparently.

WHILE SHANE HAD loved how Arden had kissed her way down his body, it was time to return the favor. Nuzzling the fragrant curve of her shoulder, he pressed butterfly kisses onto her neck while his fingers caressed her silky soft skin. She smelled fresh, probably from a recent shower, but it was more than that. The musk of her arousal hung in the air, ratcheting up the primal urgency to take her now. *Right now.* Only the civilized part of his brain kept him from grunting like a caveman, throwing her over his shoulder, and carrying her away to a nearby cave.

After the last time they'd been together when Arden had been so full of pain, he'd vowed the next time they made love it would truly be just that. Making love. No wild animals going at like they were in heat. He wanted her to know how much he truly loved and cherished her.

He nipped a path down over the soft swell of her belly and pushed her legs apart with his shoulders. Pressing open-mouthed kisses to the delicate skin of her inner thigh, he chuckled as she moved restlessly beneath him, wordlessly begging for what only he could give her.

Sliding two fingers inside her wet channel, he crooked them in a come-hither fashion and drew a long, deep moan from Arden, her legs already beginning to tremble as she neared her release.

He bent his head, giving the shiny pearl beckoning to him a lazy lick. Her hips stiffened and she whimpered his name, pleading with him to continue, which he was happy to do. This morning was about making her feel amazing and adored, and part of that was her screaming his name at the top of her lungs.

Primed and ready, it didn't take long for his teasing tongue and stroking fingers to send her over the edge. She gasped for air, her fingernails digging into his scalp but he didn't let up, his tongue sending her over a second time in a mini-climax that had her thighs clamping around his head to hold him in place.

"Shane, oh God. So good."

Her voice was barely intelligible and he couldn't hold back the swell of pride that ran through him as she lay under his body, panting and barely coherent.

And he wasn't done yet.

Hovering over her, his weight on his palms, he slowly sunk deep inside of her, savoring every second until he was in to the hilt. The tight, hot walls of her channel hugged him and he had to pause for a moment to find some modicum of control and not climax immediately like a schoolboy.

Her nails dug into his shoulders and her legs wrapped around his waist. "Please, Shane."

Her wish was his command. He began to move slowly and deliberately, pulling almost all the way out before thrusting back in, each stroke rubbing her clit. Her fingers glided down his spine and then gripped his buttocks tightly as he forced his eyes to stay open. He didn't want to miss a moment of watching Arden in the throes of passion.

Her head tossed from side to side as he pistoned into her over and over, faster and harder, until they were both close to exploding. His balls had drawn up close to his body and he couldn't hold back much longer so he reached between them, his fingers finding the center of her pleasure with unerring accuracy.

"Shane!" she called as her orgasm hit her, clenching around him until he too tumbled over, a fiery heat sweeping him from head to toe. When it was over he slumped on top of her, too drained to even move, although he was probably crushing her to death.

"I swear I'm going to roll off." He sucked oxygen into his starved and aching lungs, his limbs like lead. "Any minute now."

Giggling, she wrapped her arms around him, pressing a kiss to his sweaty chest. "I'm fine. Breathing is overrated."

With a groan, he heaved himself off and onto his back, pulling her with him and tucking her into his side, her head on his chest.

"I want to do that every night for the rest of our lives. Well, maybe not every single night but as close as we can get." He looked down at her and realized this was what he'd dreamed about all the time they'd been apart. "Basically I want to spend the rest of my life with you. Will you move in with me, Arden? Wake up with me every day? I don't think you're ready for me to propose to you, but know that's coming too."

There were logistics—like the home she was renovating and whether she'd want to live on the ranch—but those were details they could discuss later. The important thing was to make sure they were together.

But she didn't answer right away, which was making him nervous…and scared. Maybe he was moving too fast.

"I should never have left," she finally replied. "I should have stayed with you and worked on my issues but I've just been so used to having to do things on my own. I've never had anyone in my life – not even Ben – that I could trust with all my emotions. Not until you. I'm sorry, Shane. I shouldn't have put us through that."

He blew out a breath in relief. If her loner tendencies were their biggest problem then they'd be fine. "Is that a yes or a no on the moving in thing? I'm unclear."

Laughter bubbled from her lips and his heart squeezed in his chest simply listening to it, a sound he'd wondered if he'd ever hear again. He wanted to make her laugh every day.

Right along with the sex every day too.

They were going to be very busy.

"It's a yes. Absolutely yes. And you're right that I'm not ready for a marriage proposal." She leaned over and kissed him, slow and tender. "But don't wait too long. I love you."

"I love you too. We're going to be very happy, sweetheart. I promise."

Sometimes the one dream you never think will come true does just that.

Thank you for reading
Danger Incorporated – Embracing Danger
Sign up to be notified of Olivia's new releases:

oliviajaymesoptin.instapage.com

About The Author

Olivia Jaymes is a wife, mother, lover of sexy romance, and caffeine addict. She lives with her husband and son in central Florida and spends her days with handsome alpha males and spunky heroines.

She is currently working on a series of full-length novels called The Cowboy Justice Association. It's a contemporary romance series about lawmen in southern Montana who work to keep the peace but can't seem to find it in their own lives in addition to the erotic romance novella series – Military Moguls and the romantic suspense series – Danger Incorporated.

Visit Olivia Jaymes at

www.OliviaJaymes.com

Danger Incorporated

Damsel In Danger

Hiding From Danger

Indecent Danger

Discarded Heart Novella (US Kindle Only)

Cowboy Justice Association

Cowboy Command

Justice Healed

Cowboy Truth

Cowboy Famous

Cowboy Cool

Imperfect Justice

The Deputies

Justice Inked

Military Moguls

Champagne and Bullets

Diamonds and Revolvers

Caviar and Covert Ops

Emeralds, Rubies, and Camouflage